Sister Surrogate

LaChelle Weaver

BROWN GIRLS BOOKS

Houston, Texas * Washington, D.C. * Raleigh/Durham, NC

Sister Surrogate © 2016 by LaChelle Weaver

Brown Girls Books, LLC
www.BrownGirlsBooks.com

ISBN Ebook: 9781944359188
ISBN Print: 9781944359195

First Brown Girls Publishing LLC trade printing

Manufactured and Printed in the United States of America

Dedication

To my fellow Hornet and Hillside High School classmate, Tiffany Dixon Parker, my aunt Debra Faye Weaver and countless women who've battled cancer and came out victorious.

This book is for you.

Acknowledgements

This is the part of the book that I looked most forward to writing—getting to thank everyone that contributed to this labor of love either directly or indirectly. *Sister Surrogate* has been years in the making and it has not been an easy feat, but by the grace of God, who I give the highest and loudest of praises, I could not have persevered. He put this gift inside me, and guided me through the entire process from start to finish, even when I wanted to give up and quit, and when I doubted if I could really write.

To my family and friends—my incredibly talented and equally creative daughter, Janayah Lipscomb; my twin sister and womb mate, LaShawn Weaver; my beautiful nieces, Te´a Walker and Ala´ni Sanford; the sister I've always looked up to, Denita Green; the man of my dreams and my biggest supporter, Johnathan Cox; my BFFs: Marisa Watson (my best bestie), Shonnethia Johnson and Chris Mott (aka 49ers 4 Life), and my sister-friends: Michelle Chavis, Cheryl Ashford Daniels and Vanessa Johnson Sumpter. Your support has been unwavering and always encouraging and I can't tell you how grateful and blessed I am to have each and every one of you in my corner. I love you all!

To my Weaver family—much love to my mama, Donna Weaver; my grandma, Dorothy Weaver and a special thank you to my aunt, Debra Weaver whose mini library of books when I was growing up sparked my love for reading that ignited my passion for the written word. You've always been the best aunt, and I love you dearly.

A huge shout out to my work family, Team Anthony (Red Nights)— Joe Anthony, you have been one of the best supervisors I've had in my biotech career. Your support for your team and willingness to always highlight our strengths is greatly appreciated. My teammates: Jeff Chelf, our illustrious leader; Scott Paye, your wittiness always keep me laughing; Ray Joyner, you're equally funny and we're glad you're a part of our team; A special thank you to Mario Hunter—you've always been the first person I've bounced ideas for stories off of and received honest feedback. We're the original two and have seen each other grow over the years, and I'm glad you're still on this journey with me. I hope to see your passions bloom as well. Thank you also to my co-workers, Julianne Chappell (my Jules) and Mark Ellis (I miss you!). It's always easy to come to work when I have you guys as co-workers. You've all been supportive of my dream and I will always appreciate that.

My awesomely talented Sister Scribes of *The Dating Game*—Cheryl Ashford Daniels, Princess F.L. Gooden, Cherritta Smith, Natalie Woods Leffall, Minolta Walker, Loureva Watson Slade, Patrice Tartt, Kay Trina Morris, Keleigh Krigler Hadley, Gina Phillips Johnson, Gina Torres,

Tania Zayid, Marcena Hooks, Victoria Adams Kennedy, Richelle Denise and Trenekia Gilmore. I started my literary journey as a first time published author with you ladies and we skyrocketed to the top of the bestsellers list not once, but twice; not only becoming bestselling authors, but also, literary award-nominated authors. You ladies exemplify sisterhood and reinforced for me that we as women are strong in numbers, and when we work together we can do amazing things. I will forever love my Sister Scribes, my sisters in pen, and our journey as bestselling authors is only beginning.

Congratulations to my Sister Scribes Yvette Brantley, Christina Grant, Trina Charles, Cherritta Smith and Venita Alderman Sadler. Our love for the craft of writing brought us together in one or more of Victoria's classes, and now we're all published authors. I'm so proud of you ladies and looking forward to seeing you all make an impact in the literary world.

And I can't forget my hitta, my road dawg, Cassandra Baker Durham. You have an awesome way with words and every time you speak you motivate, inspire and entertain. Keep writing and continue to let your words be your ministry.

Andrea (Michelle) Mitchell, thank you for your constant encouragement and our funny conversations. You're a great writer and I can't wait for the world to read *Truth Is*. I'm blessed to not only call you my Sister Scribe, but friend as well.

Cheryl Ashford Daniels, you have been my sounding board and my biggest source of motivation. You have constantly reminded me of my gift when I was in doubt and have kept me focused. It's a blessing how easily and naturally we've connected as not only writing sisters, but great friends. Thank you for always being so supportive. I'm proud of you, and can't wait for the world to read your amazing work. Love you, my sister-friend!

To my Hillside High School classmate, Tiffany Dixon Parker and my OB/GYN, Heather Vawter, PA-C. Thank you ladies for taking the time to provide me with the medical answers I needed to tell Savannah's story accurately. I greatly appreciate the both of you.

Thank you to Lasheera Lee for giving me my first interview as a published author on your radio show Read You Later, and for the many connections you've provided me since. If it weren't for you, I wouldn't have met the amazingly talented, Rebecca Pau who designed the breathtaking cover for *Sister Surrogate*. Rebecca, you're one of the best graphic designers I've had the pleasure of working with, and you're one half of the reason why people will pick up the book to read it because of that amazing cover. Thank you so much.

To one of my favorite authors of all-time, Kimberla Lawson Roby. From the moment I picked up your first book so many years ago, I've been a die-hard fan and you're my inspiration for wanting to write in the contemporary women's fiction genre. I aspire to touch readers with my stories in the way that you have.

To the lovely ladies of Victorious Ladies Reading Book Club—thank you to my sister-friend and VLR president,

Michelle Chavis and VLR Vice President, Shavonna Futrell. You ladies have really taken book clubs to another level with your generous hospitality and appreciation for authors. You and your members have been so supportive and I greatly appreciate you. Congratulations on your upcoming endeavors and know that you will always have my support.

Thank you to the Literary Guru, Yolanda Gore for everything that you do to take authors to another level. You're a blessing.

To my Brown Girls Books family—thank you to one of the best social media managers in the business, Jason Frost; Publicist Norma Warren you are the business! Thank you for keeping BGB authors in the spotlight. And, I'm ready to shine! Thank you to my fellow writers and all of the Brown Girls Books staff that continue to make it a success.

To Jacquelin Thomas, I can't thank you enough for your mentorship and guidance in my literary journey with *Sister Surrogate*. It started with you offering me a book deal and I'm forever grateful to you for the opportunity. I hope to make you proud.

To my literary bosses, Brown Girls Books founders and trailblazing publishers, Victoria Christopher Murray and ReShonda Tate Billingsley, there are not enough words in the English language to express how grateful, honored and blessed I am to be a part of your vision. When I first met you ladies at a book signing here in Durham, NC a few years ago, I knew that I would work with you one day, and I even said that to Victoria when she came back later for her *Forever*

An Ex signing. You both inspired me to get serious about writing and I thank you for believing in me, and I can't tell you how proud I am to be a Brown Girl.

Chapter One

For Savannah Yancey, life as she knew it would never be the same. As she gripped her husband's hand, their fingers laced together in unity, tears filled her eyes. She'd just been given the worst news a woman could receive, especially a 29-year-old woman—Stage Two cervical cancer. Up until this moment, she'd held on to hope. She hadn't panicked when her Pap smear results had come back abnormal because she'd had abnormal results in the past or when she had to have a colposcopy as a result. The uneasiness crept up when she had to have a cone biopsy due to the severity of her initial biopsy results. It wasn't until she'd received a call from her OB/GYN, Dr. Pennington a few days ago, requesting that Savannah come into her office and bring someone with her, that actual fear began to set in. But she had said a prayer and hoped for a positive outcome.

Savannah listened in stunned silence as Dr. Pennington explained the results of her pathology report. Her blue eyes were sympathetic, even though her voice remained professional, but filled with compassion because she was a woman and she knew the impact it would have, especially on a woman as young as Savannah, just a few months shy of her thirtieth birthday, newly married with no children. Something she'd desired for as long as she could remember.

After leaving Dr. Pennington's office, Savannah and her husband, Julius rode in silence as she stared out the window from the passenger seat of his SUV. Her tears had dried up, but the pain she felt still lingered, which meant they could resurface at any moment. Growing up, Savannah had always been told by her now deceased mother, not to question when bad things happened because only God could provide the answer, but as she grappled with her diagnosis she couldn't help to wonder why. Why now? Why her?

Savannah thought back to her wedding day, six months ago, as she and Julius gazed into each other's eyes during their first dance together as Mr. and Mrs. Yancey.

"You take my breath away. You know that?" Julius whispered in her ear. His soft, full lips pressed against her.

Savannah beamed at his words. Her arms were wrapped snuggly around his neck.

"I didn't know that," she'd spoken, coyly in his ear in return.

"You want to know why?" he asked.

"Yes. Enlighten me, Mr. Yancey," Savannah responded.

"Because you're everything I dreamed of and more; Beautiful, intelligent and driven. I couldn't have prayed for a more perfect woman to be my wife and future baby mama of my five kids."

Savannah threw her head back in laughter. Julius was always joking with her about having a house full of beautiful, chocolate babies when in reality they'd already settled on two. With their thriving careers, two would be a reasonable number.

"We ain't the Huxtables, baby. Why don't we start with one first and see if we survive before we talk about having a brood?"

"I'm kidding, baby, but I know one thing. I'm going to enjoy myself trying. I can't wait to get you alone. You almost stopped my heart watching you walk down that aisle toward me. I love you, Mrs. Savannah Leah Yancey."

She loved hearing the sound of her married name coming from her new husband's lips.

"I love you more, Mr. Yancey," Savannah whispered back.

Julius planted a tender kiss on her lips.

"Get a room!" Julius's best man and law partner, Winston DeShazo yelled at them from behind his iPhone, a few feet away. They laughed. He was one amongst many of their guests capturing their happy moment with cameras on their smartphones.

Savannah rested the side of her head against Julius's chest as they swayed in harmony to "A Couple of Forevers" by Chrisette Michele, one of her favorite R&B singers. Savannah had felt like a princess in one of those fairytales she'd grown up reading, who had found her Prince Charming and lived happily ever after. She knew it was cliché, but it was her wedding day and there was no other way she could describe it.

But now, as she played back Dr. Pennington's words in her mind, Savannah felt like she was part of a bad dream. She tasted the saltiness of her tears, and realized she was crying again. Julius grabbed her hand from his position in the driver's seat.

"We're going to get through this, baby. Everything will be fine. Try not to worry," said Julius, taking his eyes off the road to glance at her.

He'd said the same thing earlier, right after they left Dr. Pennington's office as they walked to the car, still holding hands. Savannah didn't know if he was trying to convince her or himself. She'd remained silent like she did now because she didn't share his sentiments. How would everything be fine?

Dr. Pennington had recommended a radical hysterectomy due to her concern with where the cancer was located on her cervix along with a combination of chemotherapy and radiation. She'd be referring Savannah to a gynecologic oncologist for further testing and confirmation of her results. Savannah felt numb as her dreams of motherhood dissipated with Dr. Pennington's words. She'd never experience carrying or giving birth to a baby. That was the most difficult part of the diagnosis for her to accept, and not what she expected to hear after a few short months of marriage. She'd wanted a baby so bad; she could almost smell the sweet scent of one and feel the warmth of its soft skin against hers, which is why she hadn't wanted to waste time in trying to start a family, even though Julius felt the opposite.

The opportune time to have a baby had become a point of contention with them. Julius wanted to wait at least a year because he had plans of expanding his law practice, but Savannah had balked at the notion. Her maternal urges were growing stronger and stronger with each day, and she felt compelled to go ahead and act on them. So, every free chance they got, Savannah wanted to make love until they couldn't any longer, which sometimes lasted hours at a time with her praying for conception. And the reason she hadn't felt the vaginal bleeding she was experiencing afterward as a huge cause for concern.

She just chalked it up to too much sex, and waved it away as a minor nuisance to deal with in her ultimate goal to become pregnant. But then, it started to happen more frequently, so with Julius's insistence because he was getting freaked out about it, she had finally gone in to see Dr. Pennington, never expecting to hear that she wouldn't be able to have any children of her own since a radical hysterectomy would strip her of her uterus and cervix. It was heartbreaking.

Savannah mused over Julius's words to her on their wedding day about finding the perfect woman in her. How would he feel about her now that she couldn't give him any children?

Chapter Two

S avannah sat outside on her deck wrapped in a fleece throw, staring off at the serene lake in the distance. She'd come home from her doctor's visit, seeking solace and this was the place she often went to for relaxation that the view of Lake Norman always provided. Julius made her a cup of chai tea, sensing that she needed the time to herself while he cooked dinner. Her mind was still reeling and she felt an overwhelming sadness. Her thoughts were now on her two sisters, Bridgette and Ivy. It would be difficult to tell them her diagnosis, especially since they'd all been through this ordeal before, when their father had been diagnosed with lung cancer during the final semester of Savannah's senior year at Grambling State University.

Savannah had been devastated by the news of her father's illness because as the youngest, she'd always been Daddy's Girl and had spent so much of her young life trying to make him proud, which is why she'd become an educator. Eldridge Alston had been a history professor at Johnson C. Smith University and later, served on the Charlotte-Mecklenburg Board of Education before having to take an early retirement due to his illness. Savannah knew how proud he would be that she was now an elementary school principal. She could hear his hearty laughter and him telling her, "Good job, baby girl," which he'd always done every time she accomplished something she'd set her mind to achieve.

It had been a difficult time, especially with Savannah being so many miles away in Louisiana. She had wanted to leave school immediately to come home to North Carolina to be with her family upon learning the news of her father's illness, but her mother wouldn't hear of it. So, her sisters had dropped everything going on in their lives to come to Louisiana to be with her for a few days because she had been so shaken up. Bridgette had just given birth a few weeks prior to her twin boys, Dylan and Ryan, but packed them up and made the fourteen-hour drive from Charlotte, stopping in Atlanta to pick up Ivy, who'd been living there since graduating from Clark Atlanta University two years earlier. They'd all spent that weekend together at a hotel, comforting each other. And Savannah had gotten to bond with the babies, which she couldn't get enough of. It was one of the most memorable times with her sisters, and by the time they'd left to head back home, they'd convinced her that everything was going to be okay and that they would all get through it together. And Savannah had found comfort in their reassurances. Although she still worried about her father, she managed to finish out the semester and graduate with honors, even though her father had been too sick to attend her graduation ceremony. He died a month later.

As she watched some of her neighbors enjoying the spring evening, out on their boats, she longed for her sisters'

Chapter Three

S avannah and her sisters were gathered together in her kitchen that following Friday evening, preparing to dye eggs and bake desserts for Sunday's Easter dinner. Bridgette, the oldest, took on the baking since she did it for a living, and was the best cook out of the three of them. She was the owner of a successful bakery in Uptown Charlotte she'd named Sugar Rush. Savannah and Ivy, the middle sister were going to dye the eggs for Saturday's Easter egg hunt.

It had been hard for Savannah to put everything that she was dealing with out of her mind, but having her sisters around gave her some comfort as she expected. She'd decided to wait until after the holiday to tell them about her diagnosis. She didn't want to dampen the festive mood that the holidays always put them in when they were all together.

"Savannah. You're going to burn these eggs," Bridgette scolded, gripping the stockpot full of boiled eggs off the burner with potholders. "The water has almost boiled completely down."

Bridgette turned to face Savannah, who was prepping the dye to color the eggs. She and Ivy were sitting at the large, granite island they'd made their workspace, which they'd lined with newspaper. Small Styrofoam bowls filled with different colors of dye sat in front them. Ivy was sipping on her usual glass of red wine and humming along to R&B music that filled the large room as they worked. The sisters loved to listen to music while they cooked, something they'd grown up doing with their mother.

"Sorry," Savannah muttered.

Bridgette crossed her arms and peered at her baby sister from her place at the stove.

"Savannah? What's going on with you? You've barely uttered two words since we've been here."

"Now that you've mentioned it, Bridge, she has been a little quiet. She's probably tired from all of that bumping and grinding she's been doing with her new hubby," Ivy chimed in.

Savannah couldn't help but to chuckle at her sister's comment. Ivy always made her laugh even when she wasn't in the mood. It was good to have her home, if only for a few days. She split her time between Charlotte and Atlanta, but she hadn't been home since Christmas because of her demanding work schedule as a celebrity make-up artist, which took her all over the world.

"Maybe you're finally pregnant," Ivy said, finishing off her glass of merlot and picking up the wine bottle placed strategically next to her to replenish it.

Savannah felt like she'd punched her in the gut with those four words. She fought to hold back her tears, silently praying they wouldn't burst through to the surface because she wasn't ready to have this conversation with her sisters.

"No. That's not it. Her mood would be different," Bridgette countered, studying her baby sister as she wiped her hands with a dish towel.

"I'm fine," Savannah said, standing to her feet. "Just a little tired. It's been a long week." She needed to move around because she felt like a sitting target as Bridgette honed in on her. Bridgette would continue to badger her like she was one of those interviewers giving lie detector tests. It was in her nature as the eldest to be perceptive when it came to them. Even though they were all adults, she still felt the need to look after them, something she'd been doing since they were children and even more so after their parents died.

Savannah walked over to the refrigerator, pulled open the stainless steel double doors and retrieved a bottle of Perrier along with a small container of lemon slices. She got a glass from one of the overhead cabinets and filled it with sparkling water before dropping a few lemon slices into it and taking a long swig. Even though her back was to her sisters, she could feel Bridgette's eyes boring into her.

"Heyyy! That's my jam," Ivy declared, snapping her fingers and swaying her head to the melody of "Who Knows" by Musiq Soulchild. "This is the kind of music that you don't hear anymore."

"I have to agree with you on that, sis," said Bridgette. "Everything is B-this and Hoe-that. I miss the days when I could turn on the radio and not have to worry about what my children might hear."

Savannah was thankful for Ivy's outburst because it took Bridgette's focus off of her and back to baking. She was icing a German chocolate cake, which was one of their favorites because it was from one of their mother's many delicious recipes. It was also a specialty, a favorite at Bridgette's bakery, and always the first item on the menu to sell out.

As her sisters discussed their displeasure with the music industry, Savannah walked to the stove and picked up the large pot to drain the remaining water. A second later, she yelped out in pain, sending the pot and eggs crashing to the hardwood floor.

"Savannah, are you okay?" Bridgette asked, rushing to her sister's aide.

Savannah shook her hands from side to side in an attempt to relieve the burning sensation pulsating through her fingertips.

"Did you burn yourself? Let me see. You knew the pot was hot. I'd just taken it off the burner," Bridgette fussed.

Savannah waved her sister off. "I'm fine," she whined.

"Then why are you crying?" Bridgette asked.

Her sister's question sent a rush of more tears that she couldn't hold back. Bridgette grabbed Savannah into a tight embrace as she sobbed.

"Savannah, what's wrong, honey? And don't keep telling us you're fine because you're not," said Bridgette. "You can't lie to your sisters. We know you too well."

"Talk to us, Savannah. What is it that has you so upset? Are you and Julius having problems already?" Ivy asked, as she began cleaning up the spill. She tossed eggs that had been cracked from the fall into a nearby trashcan and grabbed the same potholders Bridgette had used earlier off the counter to pick the pot up off the floor.

The mention of her husband's name caused Savannah to cry harder because she felt guilty about everything he would have to go through.

"Come on. Let's go sit down," said Bridgette, ushering her sister back to the island and helping her back onto the barstool chair she'd been sitting on. "Ivy, hand me a paper towel, please."

Ivy did what she was asked and then joined her sisters back at the island. Bridgette handed Savannah the paper towel to wipe her face. She accepted it, but didn't use it as her tears kept falling. Ivy rubbed her back.

"It's okay, sis. We're here to support you in whatever is going on. Now, what is it?" Ivy queried, taking her seat next to Savannah. Bridgette stood at the end of the island next to her with her hand rested on her forearm. Savannah inhaled and then exhaled slowly.

"I found out yesterday that I have cervical cancer," Savannah uttered, and it felt like her words had caused her sisters to stop breathing. Except for the music playing in the background, there was a deafening silence. Savannah wasn't even sure they'd heard her until she looked from one to the other and saw the grim look on their faces. Bridgette's hand had left Savannah's arm and was now pressed to her own chest as if she was getting ready to have a heart attack.

"Are you sure?" Ivy managed to say, her voice cracking. Savannah nodded.

"I'm so sorry, baby sis," Bridgette finally said, placing her hand back on Savannah's arm. Her eyes were full of tears.

Savannah dropped her head as more tears seeped from her own eyes.

"Everything is going to be all right, Savannah. We have to trust in our Lord and Savior that everything will be," said Bridgette, wiping her tears.

They'd all been through this before with their father when he was diagnosed with lung cancer, but never imagined they'd be dealing with it with one of them. Savannah was so young and had so much life to live.

"What did the doctors say?" Ivy asked, fighting back her own tears.

"I had an abnormal Pap smear a few weeks ago. I went in to have a colposcopy and then a cone biopsy and the results revealed that I have Stage Two cervical cancer."

Bridgette gasped, causing tears to spill from Ivy's eyes, but Savannah continued. "I see an oncologist in a few weeks, but more than likely, I'll have to undergo a hysterectomy, which means my hopes of giving my husband a child are null and void," said Savannah, as a new wave of tears sprang to her eyes.

"Let's try not to get ahead of ourselves until we know a little bit more about this," said Bridgette. "God always has the last say."

"Wait a minute. Isn't cervical cancer caused by a sexually transmitted disease?" asked Ivy, her face scrunched up like there was a stench wafting in the air. "H-P something."

"HPV," Savannah muttered. She'd had the same reaction when Dr. Pennington mentioned that the virus was contracted through sexual contact, but she assured Savannah that HPV was nothing nasty or dirty or anything that she should feel ashamed about. It was as common as a cold, and more than 80 percent of women contracted it during their lifetime without ever knowing it. For most women, it went away on its own. But for some, as in Savannah's case, if it remained undetected it could develop into cervical cancer. She'd been lax in getting her annual pelvic exams, and now it was going to cost her. Big time.

"Did Julius give you this?" Ivy demanded. Her voice now angry and her eyes narrowed.

"Ivy, would you stop it? This isn't the time," Bridgette admonished, glaring at Ivy who in return rolled her eyes.

"It's okay, Bridgette," Savannah said, wiping her face with the paper towel Bridgette had given her. She explained what Dr. Pennington had relayed to her about HPV.

"So, I have no way of knowing if I got it from Julius or not. There's no HPV test for men, and we've both had other sexual partners during our lifetime, so I'll never know, but honestly, I couldn't care less about how I got it. That's the least of my worries."

"I know, sis. I'm sorry. I hate that this is happening to you. You don't deserve this," said Ivy, hugging Savannah.

"No matter the outcome, Savannah. We're going to help you get through this. We've been through our share of ordeals, but we always come out victorious because we've always had each other to lean on. And this won't be any different," said Bridgette, patting Savannah's hand. Savannah managed to give her sister a weak smile.

"I'll try my best to be here as much as I can, but you know I'm always just a phone call away," Ivy added.

"I appreciate the both of you so much. I don't know what I'd do without you two. I love you, sissies," Savannah said, referring to the childhood name they still called each other.

"We love you, too," Bridgette and Ivy said in unison.

"And please, promise me that you'll get your annual pelvic exams. I know we're all busy, but it's so important. I don't want you to end up like me. I hadn't had one in two years," Savannah said.

"I have been since I've always had irregular periods," said Ivy.

"I've been getting mine, too," Bridgette said. "As a matter of fact, I have an appointment coming up with Dr. Pennington next week."

"Well, it makes me feel better hearing that you both have. I should've been doing the same. But, I can't focus on that now," Savannah mused.

"Savannah, everything will be okay. I really believe that," Bridgette said, hugging her. Then Ivy wrapped her arms around them both.

As the three sisters formed a group hug, Savannah fought back more tears. She was drained from crying, but now her mind was on her mortality. She didn't want to think about the possibility of leaving her sisters behind because they'd always been a trio, but it could happen. People died from cancer every day, their father had. She couldn't help thinking about this possibly being her plight as well. She didn't want to die. There was so much she wanted to do.

Chapter Four

"I see you still haven't learned to practice any tact," Bridgette said, keeping her eyes on the road ahead of her as she steered her Suburban down the freeway.

"I beg your pardon?" Ivy asked, her tone incredulous as she peered at her sister from the passenger seat. She'd been staring out the window, her thoughts on Savannah. Both of them had been silent up until this point. Ivy was certain Bridgette had been deep in her own thoughts about their sister's devastating revelation, so she was caught off guard by her sudden outburst.

"You don't see anything wrong with how you came at Savannah? She's received probably the worst news a woman can get and all you could think to ask her was how she got it? Really, Ivy?" Bridgette chided, her voice just as incredulous. "You never cease to amaze me with what manages to come out of your mouth." Bridgette shook her head.

"Did you miss the part where I apologized? Don't start with me, Bridgette. I'm not here for it," Ivy said, rolling her eyes and focusing them back on the tall buildings that made up the Charlotte skyline, hovering above them outside the window.

"It's not enough for you to keep apologizing after you say things, Ivy. Once they come out of your mouth, the sting of your words still linger. Remember that the next time you decide to run your mouth," Bridgette said.

Ivy glared at her sister.

"Do you really think my intent was to hurt Savannah? She's my sister too, in case you forgot, and I love her just as much as you do. It was a valid question whether you felt it was or not, and once she explained it, I had a better understanding. So, get off my case and off your throne, Queen Bee. It's annoying." Ivy returned her attention back outside the window. She hated when Bridgette was condescending. That was her biggest pet peeve with her older sister other than her nosiness.

"You know what, Ivy? It must be really nice in the world you live in where you can do whatever you want, when you want and not have to worry about much of anything else besides what new pair of Christian Louboutins to buy or whatever designer handbag is in this season," Bridgette retorted.

"What's your point?" Ivy challenged, facing Bridgette again.

"Well, you've always been pretty vocal about never wanting to be married or have any children. You've also plunged yourself into a career that would make it virtually impossible anyway, so it makes you insensitive to anyone that desires either. But, I would expect you to be more considerate when that person is your own sister," Bridgette said. "It wouldn't hurt you to show a little sensitivity sometimes."

Ivy was glad that they were just a few exits away from her condo because it would get ugly if she had to be in the car with her older sister much longer. She didn't want to go there with Bridgette. Despite their disagreements, and they'd had many over the years because that's what sisters did, she had the utmost respect for her.

As the eldest, Bridgette had always put their needs before her own. She would go to battle for them, and she had the scars to prove it. She was the epitome of selflessness, something Ivy admired about Bridgette because if she was being honest, it wasn't exactly a quality she possessed, and she didn't make any apologies about that.

"So, I chose to seek a career that I love. We all did. And, just because I didn't choose to be tied down to a man and some rugrats, that doesn't make me a bad person, so stop trying to make it seem that way."

"You see what I mean about practicing some tact? You just called my kids rugrats, even if you weren't intending to," Bridgette said, shaking her head as she turned on her signal to take the upcoming exit to Ivy's condo building.

Ivy waved her hand, dismissing Bridgette's comment. "You're being ridiculous, Bridgette. You know that's not what I meant. I love my nephews. You know that."

"Again, you never *mean* to say anything that you do," Bridgette remarked, rolling her eyes.

Ivy was about to say something regarding her sister's nasty tone, but decided to keep her comments to herself since everything she'd said thus far, Bridgette seemed to want to counter. She didn't have the energy to keep going back and forth with her. They'd just received unsettling news about their sister, but here they were arguing. They rode the rest of the way in silence.

Chapter Five

Ivy was almost regretting coming home. Back in Atlanta, she'd been looking forward to spending time with her sisters and enjoying the Easter weekend with them. She hadn't seen them since the Christmas holidays, and with her traveling so much, she rarely got to come home. So, it always felt good to be around them, especially since she didn't have anyone in Atlanta. Despite their differences on occasion, they were close.

That's why it pained her that cancer was intruding upon their family once again. It wasn't fair. Savannah didn't deserve this.

Just six months ago, she and Bridgette were giving their baby sister away to the man she was destined to spend the rest of her life with at her wedding, joking with her about all of the chocolate babies she was going to have with Julius because that's all she talked about. For as long as she could remember, that had been Savannah's favorite topic of conversation.

Ivy chuckled when she thought back to the Cabbage Patch dolls Savannah called her babies that she would push around in a little pink stroller with a purple handle. One was a bald-headed boy named Mickey Wade and the other was a girl with two pigtails with brown yarn for hair named Ramona Jill. They'd belonged to Bridgette first and she'd gladly passed them down to Savannah since Ivy had never been into playing with dolls; she liked to dress up in her mother's clothes and heels instead. She'd gotten into trouble so many times for playing around in her mother's make-up and jewelry.

Ivy wiped tears from her eyes as she sat propped up in her bed with pillows behind her, thinking about how happy their childhood had been, growing up together in the Alston household.

Eldridge and Aretha Alston were married over thirty-five years, instilling in their three girls the importance of family and education, two things they were passionate about. It was an unspoken rule that they would all go to college and make something of themselves. And they all had.

She always took comfort in knowing that they'd made their parents proud. That's why she hated when they fought. Her parents never liked it, and she knew they'd be disappointed to see her and Bridgette always at it, especially now that their baby girl was going through such a difficult time. They'd expect them to put their differences aside and band together like they had when they'd lost them. Ivy wanted that to, but Bridgette made it hard sometimes. It was like she still looked at she and Savannah as still being those little girls she'd grown up looking after.

Ivy didn't understand why she always felt the need to chastise her like she was one of her children. So what she didn't want a husband and children? That was her choice, as there were many women in the world who felt that way. She never made her sisters feel bad about the choices they made or how they chose to live their lives. They were all different in that way, and Ivy respected that, and Bridgette needed to do the same.

She grabbed her iPhone off the nightstand to call Savannah to check up on her.

"How you doing, Bubbling Brown Sugar?" Ivy asked when she heard her sister's voice on the other end, using the nickname she'd given her when they were kids because of her outgoing personality and lustrous skin tone.

"Hey, Ivy League. I'm doing okay," said Savannah, her own nickname for Ivy who she always said was in a league of her own. "Just watching TV and waiting on Julius to get home."

"He still ain't home yet? It's almost nine thirty," said Ivy, glancing at the clock on her nightstand. She knew her brother-in-law was a workaholic, and she respected his hustle because her sister didn't want for much of anything, but now she was sick, so the game had changed.

"He's on the way."

Ivy could detect the displeasure in her sister's voice, even though she was trying to be understanding, but Ivy knew it bothered her. Savannah wasn't confrontational unlike herself.

"Savannah, it's too early in your marriage for you to already be feeling a certain way about your husband's actions. Far be it from me to offer anyone marital advice, but it may be time to have a talk with Julius, especially after what you told us today about your diagnosis. I'll leave it at that because unlike your other sister, I try and stay out of people's business. Speaking of which, we got into it on the way home from your house."

"What happened?" Savannah asked.

"Basically, Bridgette being Bridgette. On her high horse as usual. But, I want to apologize again if I hurt your feelings in any way. I guess sometimes I don't think before I say things." Ivy thought about what Bridgette said to her earlier, and she felt bad, hoping she hadn't offended Savannah.

"It's okay, Ivy. I know you didn't mean anything by it. Are you two going to be okay though?"

"Girl, you know how we do. We'll be fine," said Ivy, waving her hand in dismissal as if her sister could see her.

"I know, but we both know how Bridgette is. Maybe you should call her tonight before it gets too late and apologize."

"And what makes you think that I'm the one who needs to apologize?"

Ivy had thought about calling Bridgette to smooth things over, but decided to let her cool off. When Bridgette was in her feelings about something it was best to let her be. Hopefully, she'd be in a better mood tomorrow. If she weren't, then that would be her problem. Ivy was only here for a few days anyway, so she wasn't going to worry too much about it.

"That's not what I'm saying. I just think whatever it was it's not worth the discord. You two always make things bigger than what they need to be," said Savannah.

"Savannah, don't get in the middle. It's not your battle. Besides, you have far more to worry about than a silly, little argument between Bridgette and me." Ivy let out a yawn. The Ambien she'd taken before her shower combined with the glasses of red wine she'd consumed at Savannah's were starting to wear her down. Her eyes were growing heavier by the minute.

"Fine. I'll leave it alone and let you guys work it out on your own. I just don't want you all having beef with one another, especially not now," said Savannah and Ivy could hear the weariness in her voice. She was always put in the position of being the peacemaker between she and Bridgette.

"Who are we? Biggie and Tupac? There's no beef," said Ivy, and Savannah chuckled. "It's all good."

Ivy saw an incoming text message flash at the top of the screen of her iPhone from Kean Hawkins, a NBA player with the Philadelphia 76ers. She'd been seeing him on and off for about a year whenever he came to Atlanta to visit his family or had a game there. He had a young daughter who lived there as well.

"Hey baby," Ivy heard Savannah say, which meant Julius had come home.

"Your hubby finally brought his hind parts home, I see. So, I'll let you go. I love you and I'll see you tomorrow," said Ivy, stifling another yawn.

"Love you too, sissy. Good night."

After ending her call with her sister, Ivy tapped the screen of her phone to pull up her messages.

Hey pretty lady. In the ATL. Playing the Hawks tomorrow. Be here 'til Sunday. Want to come to the game? We can have dinner after.

A smile spread across Ivy's face. It would've been good to see Kean because it had been a few months since she'd seen him last, but between basketball season and all the travel time she burned flying from one city to the next, it was a miracle they got to see each other at all. But, the great thing about them not being in a relationship—at least a committed one is it wasn't an issue for either of them. They just enjoyed each other's company when they got the chance to.

In the Queen City with my family. Talk tomorrow, after game? Ivy responded with a few, quick taps on the screen.

He replied with a sad face emoji. And then, *Look forward to hearing that cute, 'lil country voice. Haha!!*

Really? I know you're not talking with that deep Nawlins drawl. Boy, bye! Ivy typed as she chuckled. They exchanged a few more playful text messages before finalizing plans to talk the next day.

Ivy was drained from being on planes over the past month, and then coming home to find out about her sister's cervical cancer diagnosis that she couldn't think about anything but sleeping. She put her iPhone in Do Not Disturb mode and said her nightly prayers, especially for Savannah before snuggling under the softness of the down comforter. It felt good to be sleeping in her own bed instead of in a hotel. She didn't care how many stars they were rated or how expensive, there was nothing like being in your own space. With everything that was on her mind, she would welcome sleep tonight. She thought about one of her mother's favorite scriptures, "Weeping may endure for a night, but joy cometh in the morning."

Chapter Six

Bridgette moaned as her husband massaged her shoulders and then traveled slowly down her back. Her eyes were closed as Nick's strong hands kneaded her soft flesh, and she could feel some of the stress of her day releasing from her body.

"Baby, that feels so good. Those hands have been touched by God," Bridgette cooed. Nick chuckled. Bridgette lay in their bed on her stomach as he straddled her from behind, her head resting comfortably on a pillow. She'd just enjoyed a much-needed, relaxing, hot bath and this massage from her husband was like one of her delectable desserts from Sugar Rush, sweet and satisfying.

Bridgette had been feeling some type of way since learning about her sister's cancer diagnosis that day along with arguing with Ivy. It hadn't been the day she'd been looking forward to, which was spending time with her baby sisters. It was unimaginable that their day would end the way it had with them all in tears.

"I know it's difficult, but I want you to try and relax," said Nick.

"Now, that's going to be easier said than done, honey. I still can't believe it. Savannah is so young. I'm worried how this will affect her. So many of her dreams have been about having a husband and children."

"I'm sure she'll be okay. Savannah's a trooper. And, she has the support of family and Jules. He's a great guy," said Nick.

"He is. I won't argue with you about that," said Bridgette. She felt her husband's hands relax. She turned her head to look back at him. "Why'd you stop?" Bridgette asked. Nick had moved from her to his side of the bed. Bridgette turned her body to get a full view of him as he lay on his back with his hands behind his head and his eyes closed.

"I feel a 'but' coming on. What's on your mind, Bridgette?" Nick inquired.

"A lot is on my mind, honey. My baby sister has cancer," Bridgette responded. She was propped up on her elbow with the side of her face resting in her open palm.

Nick opened his eyes and gazed into hers. "I can see that. I can also see your brain cells working overtime in your head. You're already trying to figure out how you can try and fix it," said Nick.

"That's my baby sister, so of course I'll do whatever I can to help."

Nick grunted. Bridgette sat up in bed and peered at her husband. She'd been married to him for ten years, so she knew it meant he was frustrated.

"What is it, Nick? Just say it," Bridgette implored.

"Look. It's been a long day for the both of us. Let's just get some shut eye and pick this up in the morning," said Nick.

her marriage. Could she and Julius survive such a blow so early in their marriage not even yet a year in? She loved her husband and wanted them to be able to go the distance, but what if Julius couldn't really accept her infertility? They hadn't talked about it much, but that was more on Savannah's end. He acted as if he was supportive, and Savannah felt it was genuine, but what about later on? How was her barrenness going to affect him? Would he question his own manhood like she was questioning her womanhood? She was going to be stripped of the one thing that society said made her a woman, and that was hard for her to accept. What if he couldn't handle it or even worse, sought out another woman who could give him what Savannah couldn't?

Those thoughts had been whirling around in Savannah's mind since seeing her oncologist, Dr. Stein. They were all consuming. Even though she spent most of her time in bed, minus a few showers. Savannah rarely slept. She'd pretend to be asleep when Julius came into their bedroom to avoid conversation, and though she knew that didn't fool him most of the time, he didn't prod her. She'd feel the soft touch of his full lips on her cheek and then the warmth of his breath as he whispered into her ear that he loved her, and then when he left out of the room, her tears would fall like they were doing now.

Savannah sobbed for their marriage, for the loss of the baby they couldn't have and for the arduous battle ahead of her to rid her body of the cancer that had invaded it and turned their fairytale into a nightmare.

Chapter Eight

Bridgette thought about her husband's warning to let Savannah and Julius handle her recent diagnosis, but it was fleeting, especially since Savannah hadn't been taking any of her calls and was refusing visitors. Nick knew her well enough to know that when it came to her sisters she would always make sure they were okay, even when they acted as if they didn't want her to. Their mother would've done the same had she been alive, and she'd expect Bridgette to do the same. It was obvious Savannah needed her big sister.

As she made the drive to Savannah's house, she thought back to the day her parents had brought her home from the hospital as the newest addition to the Alston family.

Ten-year-old Bridgette hadn't been at all thrilled about another baby being in the house because she already had then two-year-old Ivy to contend with. Ivy was going through the dreaded Terrible Twos and was annoying. Bridgette often had to look after her while their mother was cooking or gardening or doing some other household chore because Ivy was a handful. Much like she was now as an adult. She'd pull things out of place, put any and everything into her mouth and then attempt to throw a temper tantrum, that was unless their father was around because he'd put a quick stop to it with his famous stern look.

Although Ivy grated her nerves, the toddler adored her big sister and Bridgette wouldn't have admitted it then, but she felt the same about her. Anywhere Bridgette was in the house, that's where Ivy wanted to be also, and when Bridgette wasn't in her eyesight, she went all over the house looking for her and calling out for "Bre Bre". So, having another little girl in the house had taken some getting used to on both of their parts.

Ivy was jealous because she had to share attention with a new baby and she wanted nothing to do with Savannah the first few months of her life. If she saw Bridgette with her, Ivy would cry and pout with her little arms folded and a scowl on her face and then yell, "My Bre Bre. Not yours. Don't like you!"

Bridgette chuckled at the memory. She'd had to break up many fights between the two of them growing up, but now Savannah was the one breaking up the fights between Bridgette and Ivy.

Bridgette pulled into the driveway of her younger sister's two-story, brick home and parked her SUV in front of one of the two car garages. She turned off the ignition and grabbed her purse, flinging it on her shoulder and picked up the bright-pink box with her bakery's logo displayed on the top that was resting on the passenger's seat. It housed one of her famous sweet potato pies Savannah loved so much. It would be a peace offering for driving out to her sister's house unannounced, but the way she saw it, she didn't have much of a choice since Savannah was ignoring her.

Bridgette pressed the lighted doorbell, sending a melodic chime on the other side of the front door. Seconds later, Julius appeared at the entrance, a dishtowel in his hands. The smell of something savory permeated out onto the porch where Bridgette stood. Her brother-in-law was obviously whipping up one of his delicious specialty dishes. Along with his dark chocolate good looks and intelligence, his excellent culinary skills had obviously sealed it for her baby sister. Savannah wasn't much of a cook, neither was Ivy for that matter, so it had to be a plus to have a man that loved to. Bridgette could only wish that Nick would step in front of a stove.

"Bridgette? What are you doing here? Did Savannah call you?" Julius asked, a bit of surprise in his voice.

"No, which is the reason I'm here. She still hasn't been taking any of my calls. I just need to lay eyes on her and make sure she's okay," said Bridgette.

Julius had ushered her into the foyer and shut the front door behind her.

"Did I catch you guys at a bad time? Smells like you're cooking something delicious."

"I've got a veggie lasagna baking in the oven. It's one of Savannah's favorites. I'm hoping it'll entice her to want to finally eat something. You're welcome to stay for dinner," said Julius.

"It smells divine and thank you for the offer, but I'm not going to stay too long. I've got to get home to cook dinner myself. I just want to check on my sister and then I'll be on my way."

"Sweet potato pie?" Julius asked, pointing to the box.

Bridgette looked down at her hands as if she'd just realized she was carrying it. "Yes. I guess we had the same thought," said Bridgette, referring to Savannah's recent non-eating habit.

"Here, I'll stick it in the fridge." Julius took the box from her. He put his nose to it and sniffed. "It sure smells good."

Bridgette followed her brother-in-law to the kitchen.

"Can I get you something to drink?" He opened the fridge and slid the box onto a shelf before closing it. "I'm going to make Savannah a cup of chai tea. Would you like a cup?"

"Sure. I'll take a cup." Bridgette removed her purse from her shoulder and placed it on the large, granite island. Julius must have been in the process of making a salad before answering the door. There was a large, wooden salad bowl sitting on the other end of the island with tomatoes, cucumbers, carrots and a bag of mixed greens next to it.

Bridgette took a seat on one of the bar stool chairs and watched her brother-in-law fill a white teakettle with water before placing it on one of the burners on the stove. After turning it on, he washed his hands at the built-in sink on the island, grabbed a paper towel from a nearby roll and dried his hands.

"Are you coming straight from work?" he queried, tossing the crumpled paper towel into a nearby trashcan.

Bridgette nodded. She was wearing a pink shirt that also had her bakery logo stitched on the front. "Yes. It's been so busy. It's wedding and baby season," said Bridgette, and then quickly regretted her last two words. She and Julius gave each other an awkward look. "I'm sorry, Julius. I didn't mean to mention…"

Julius silenced her by putting up his hands.

"There's no need for you to apologize, Bridge. It's okay."

"I know it's a sensitive subject and I don't want to say anything that could hurt you or Savannah."

Julius sliced the vegetables for the salad on a cutting board.

"It's fine, Bridgette. Really. You don't have to tiptoe around anything with me. You know we can talk about anything. We're family."

Bridgette smiled. She was glad she hadn't offended her brother-in-law because that was the last thing she wanted to do, especially since she'd scolded Ivy for doing that very thing. "I know. How are you though? I haven't had a chance to talk with you much since we were all here a few weekends ago for Easter," said Bridgette.

Julius shrugged. "I'm doing okay under the circumstances. I'm more worried about Savannah."

"We all are. I can't begin to imagine what she's going through emotionally. I still don't think I've completely processed it all myself. I guess I've been going through these few weeks on autopilot. It's the only way I can explain it."

"Oh, I definitely feel where you're coming from. It's hard to focus on much of anything when the person you love the most is going through something so traumatic," said Julius, using the knife he'd cut vegetables up with to move them off the cutting board, dumping them on top of the mixed greens already in the salad bowl.

Bridgette could tell he loved being in the kitchen. He moved about the space with as much ease as being in a courtroom. He could've been a chef if he wasn't a successful attorney. Just then, a whistle hissed from the teakettle. Julius retrieved two mugs from an overhead cabinet and placed a tea bag in each, filling them with the scalding water. He handed one to Bridgette. She thanked him before blowing inside the mug and then taking a sip.

"Do you want to come on up to the bedroom while I take this to Savannah?" he asked. Bridgette rose from her seat. "Let me do it. I can check in on her while you're finishing up down here," Bridgette offered.

A few minutes later, she'd made her way up to their bedroom, gripping a mug in each of her hands. Savannah was just as surprised to see her as Bridgette was by her appearance. There was no nice way to put it. Her baby sister looked a hot mess. She was glad Ivy wasn't there to tell her so because there was no doubt in Bridgette's mind that is exactly what she would've done since the space between her brain and her mouth lacked a filter.

Savannah was sitting up in bed with pillows propped behind her and a remote control in her hand, blindly flipping through TV channels when Bridgette entered the bedroom. The scowl fixed on her face told Bridgette that Savannah wasn't too happy about her being there, but she didn't care. Savannah would have to get over it.

"What are you doing here?" Savannah demanded.

Her tone was snappish, but Bridgette didn't let it deter her. She'd come to lay eyes on her sister and now that she had, she was mad at herself for not coming sooner. Savannah needed a good talking to and she was going to give it to her.

"Well, if you'd taken my calls I wouldn't have to be here. So, now that I am get used to it," said Bridgette, her own tone forceful.

Savannah had to know that she wasn't there to play nice with her. She needed to pull herself out of the rut she'd climbed in. She wasn't going to have her going into the hospital sooner than she had to. Unfortunately, there would be enough of that to come.

"Julius made you a cup of tea," said Bridgette, extending one of the mugs out to Savannah after she'd made her way over to the bed.

"Did Julius call you to come here?" Savannah huffed, ignoring Bridgette's offer.

"No. I just told you why I'm here. And from the looks of it, not a moment too soon," Bridgette said, placing the mugs on the nightstand. She surveyed her sister. Savannah looked like she'd aged five years since the last time Bridgette had seen her, which was two weeks ago. Dark circles plagued her eyes and her hair looked like it hadn't seen a comb in weeks.

"Savannah, I get that you're hurting, but you can't shut out the very people who are trying to support you. We're your family and we love you."

Bridgette stood with her hands on her hips looking at Savannah who'd turned her attention back to the TV, dismissing her. Bridgette sighed and then sat down at the edge of the bed. She patted the top of the duvet where Savannah's feet were.

"Sweetie, look at me," Bridgette murmured, but Savannah continued to ignore her. "Savannah, I'm not going to go away. You know that I'll sit here all night if I have to. So, stop acting like a brat. That's Ivy's thing. Not yours," said Bridgette, but Savannah still didn't budge. "All right. Fine. Suit yourself." Bridgette rose from the bed and walked over to the opposite side. She removed her red Toms and climbed in the empty space next to her sister.

"Bridgette, I'm not in the mood for company, so please just go on home," said Savannah, finally breaking her silent treatment.

"As I told you before, I will once you talk to me." Bridgette scooted closer to Savannah's side. "And the first thing I'd like to know is why are you trying to starve yourself?"

"Stop being dramatic. I just haven't had an appetite lately. There's nothing wrong with that. I'll eat when I feel like it," Savannah snapped.

"And when was the last time you *felt* like it?"

"Bridgette, leave me alone. I don't want to talk about this. I'm not Dylan or Ryan. You're their mother, not mine."

"And I'm not trying to be, Savannah. I'm only trying to look out for your best interests. And I have to say, I don't like what I'm seeing here. It seems to me that you've already given up the battle before it's even started. That's not the baby sister I know."

"Yeah, well, sorry to disappoint you, but you're not the one with cancer in her body. I am. So, excuse me for not acting how you think I should act."

Bridgette ignored her sister's angry tone. She was just glad that Savannah was finally talking to her and hopefully getting out some of those emotions she'd been bottling up inside of her.

"Savannah. I won't even fix my mouth to say I understand what you're going through mentally and emotionally because I don't. But, I do know that you have a strong support system around you, including me and you don't have to fight this thing alone. We've been through some tough times and this won't be any different. Let us help you, honey," Bridgette said, placing her hand on top of her sister's.

Savannah remained silent, but there were tears running down the side of her face as she stared at the TV. Bridgette thought that her words had gotten through to her sister, but then Bridgette noticed a baby commercial was on, advertising diapers. Bridgette scooted closer to Savannah so that they were hip to hip and placed an arm around her, pulling Savannah's head down on her shoulder. Savannah didn't resist or put up an argument. She released her pain onto her big sister's shoulder.

"I love you, Savannah," Bridgette murmured as she rested her head on top of Savannah's. "We're going to get through this. I promise."

Chapter Nine

After leaving Savannah's house, as Bridgette cooked dinner for her family and they sat down to eat, she didn't participate in much of the conversation that was going on between her boys and their father because she couldn't rid her mind of the heartbreaking image of that baby commercial and Savannah's reaction to it.

Sleep didn't come easy that night either. Bridgette tossed and turned until she'd finally got up at three-thirty so she wouldn't disturb Nick, to make herself a glass of warm milk like her mother did when they were growing up and couldn't sleep. She went into the family room and made herself comfortable on the red leather sectional, one of her favorite accents to the room other than the red wall. She had quite a few red items displayed throughout the house, an ode to her sorority, Delta Sigma Theta.

When Bridgette turned on the large, flat screen TV over the fireplace, that same baby commercial came on as if haunting her. She hurried to change the channel, but it only deepened the angst she already felt. She thought about Savannah crying on her shoulder like a scared little girl and Bridgette couldn't hold back her own tears. She hadn't cried while she was comforting her baby sister because she needed to be strong for her, but being alone made it easier for her to release her own pain.

It was hard seeing their father deteriorate from cancer and then a few years later, have their mother suffer a brain aneurysm and never recover afterwards. That had been difficult enough, but seeing her baby sister having to go through this was the most painful for Bridgette because she herself was a mother and she knew that being able to have children was a blessing and one of the greatest gifts a woman could give not only herself, but to her husband as well. And both Savannah and Julius deserved that.

Now, here it was the next morning and as she sat at her desk in her office at the bakery, a tear rolled off her face and splattered onto her desk, snapping Bridgette out of her gloomy thoughts. She plucked a tissue from the box sitting nearby and wiped her eyes and face. She needed to get herself together for the long day ahead of her.

Wednesday was truly Hump Day for Bridgette and her staff, and she always came into the bakery early before everyone arrived to get all of her administrative duties out of the way so she could focus on baking. They would be prepping for three weddings and a handful of birthday parties for the upcoming weekend and she had two cake tastings on the schedule for today as well. Not to mention the daily heavy traffic of customers that came through for their favorite sweet treats. Sugar Rush was steadily thriving and Bridgette couldn't be happier, but Nick was beginning to complain more than ever about her "trying to do too much" as he always put it.

While she did spend a great deal of her time during the week at the bakery, Bridgette did that to ensure her weekends would be free for her family. Occasionally, she did have to make a personal appearance for a special function, but she had a trusted and dedicated staff that was a key part of Sugar Rush's success and she could rely on them to keep things running smoothly during her absence. Bridgette would really need to count on them more than she ever had to before if what she was planning to do actually happened.

She knew Nick wouldn't be happy about it, at least at first, but he loved Savannah just as much as she did and the two of them had always been close, joking around with each other and teasing one another, so Bridgette was hoping that would be enough for Nick to show empathy toward her baby sister and concede with her plan.

Bridgette had been sitting at her desk with her usual venti-white chocolate-mocha-Frappuccino from the Starbucks around the corner and her favorite inspirational music station playing over the surround sound system. She really needed both that morning, especially since she hadn't been able to get back to sleep after getting up so early and feeling emotionally spent about her sister. She'd been glued in front of the large screen of her iMac since arriving at Sugar Rush around seven o'clock, after dropping her boys off at before school care. The bakery didn't open until nine, so that gave her a few hours to herself to do the things she needed to do in preparation for the day, but she hadn't gotten much of it done. Her focus was on something far more important to her at the moment.

"We could definitely do this if we act fast and go ahead and extract Savannah's eggs, but I don't know how Julius would feel about having to ejaculate into a cup," she said, frowning and as if someone else was in the room with her. Bridgette scrolled further down the screen, engrossed in the article she'd been reading.

"Twelve thousand dollars? Sweet Baby Jesus," she exclaimed, shaking her head.

No wonder celebrities are the only ones I've ever heard of doing this. This whole surrogacy thing is expensive. Good Lord! She thought.

Bridgette didn't know anyone personally who'd been through it, but she knew it was very popular with celebrity women who wanted to maintain their body images. In particular, she'd remembered Angela Bassett hiring a surrogate to carry and birth her two children, and even though Angela was one of her favorite actresses and she didn't know her personal medical history, Bridgette also remembered thinking how vain it seemed, but as she sat staring at the computer screen, she realized what a blessing it could be, especially for someone in Savannah's position.

Despite the astronomical costs, the few articles she'd read about surrogacy, in particular, gestational surrogacy, which would be applicable to Savannah's situation, had been encouraging. Physically, Bridgette felt that she was a viable candidate to carry a baby for her sister, and it filled her with an abundance of hope that she could potentially give her sister the ultimate gift that she could ever give—the gift of life.

Chapter Ten

S avannah felt like her tear ducts should be dried up from all of the tears she'd shed over the past few weeks. She wiped her eyes with her hands, and stared at her sister with shock and a bit of confusion. Savannah couldn't believe the words that had come out of Bridgette's mouth as they sat outside on her deck with the beautiful view of Lake Norman. Spring was in full effect, and despite the pollen, the weather was pleasant. It was the first time Savannah had been out of her bedroom and out of the house for that matter, and if it wasn't for Bridgette's nagging, that's where she would've stayed. So, to shut her up, Savannah relented when she suggested they have the lunch she'd brought with her out there.

Once again, Bridgette had come over unannounced, saying that she had something important to talk to her about. Savannah knew it must have been if she was there during a workday. And even though she still didn't have much of an appetite, Savannah had been committing herself to eating something even if it was just a piece of fruit. She agreed that she needed to keep her strength up for her upcoming surgery. It had taken some urging from Bridgette after she'd cried on her shoulder a few days ago, but Savannah had conceded.

It was something about her big sister comforting her that lifted Savannah's spirit some. Bridgette had that affect sometimes. You could be annoyed with her one minute and then appreciate her the next. There was something about a sister's love, and that was the only way Savannah could explain it. And here she was again, offering a kind of love that only a sister could give.

"I really don't know what to say, Bridgette. I'm at a loss for words," said Savannah. They'd been eating salads and drinking glasses of fresh mint and ginger lemonade, one of many recipes Savannah was always trying her hand at. She had gotten it off of Pinterest. She was good at making drinks, but not so much with cooking. Bridgette was always joking that their mother would be appalled at how bad she and Ivy cooked.

"I know this is a bit sudden, but I've thought long and hard about this Savannah. And, I've done a lot of research over the last few days. I'd really love to do this for you and Julius. You two deserve this more than anyone I know," said Bridgette. She'd rested her fork in her container and was looking at Savannah with a serious expression.

"I don't know, Bridgette. As much as I want a baby, I don't know about this. That's such a huge sacrifice and I'm not sure how comfortable I'd be with you doing that," said Savannah, her voiced filled with hesitation. She dabbed at her moist eyes with a napkin.

"I know it's a lot to consider, but think about the end result. That beautiful, chocolate bundle of joy you and Julius have been talking about since he proposed to you. I want to do it, Savannah."

Savannah was filled with a myriad of emotions, which had become commonplace over the past few weeks. She was happy, but apprehensive at the same time. She was sad, but now, optimistic and hopeful again. Honestly, she'd never even considered surrogacy. She didn't know anything about it other than what she'd seen on TV and she would've never paid some stranger to carry her baby. She knew that there were cases where that hadn't ended well for the intended parents, and she couldn't imagine being that mother who placed all her hope on another woman fulfilling her dreams of motherhood, and then snatching it away because she'd had a sudden change of heart. It was unimaginable, but now here her sister was offering her a similar dream.

Savannah had vaguely remembered her oncologist, Dr. Stein mentioning something about having her eggs frozen as an option to her impending infertility, since they intended to save her ovaries to reduce her chances of being thrown into menopause, but she'd completely shut down after he'd given her the final diagnosis. So, she hadn't been able to hear much of anything else thereafter. She'd completely shut down and had been that way until now. Bridgette had sparked that maternal feeling in her again that she thought would be forever extinguished when doctors removed her uterus in a few weeks.

"Are you sure about this, Bridgette? What did Nick say about this?"

Bridgette averted her eyes momentarily and then looked back at Savannah.

"So, you haven't even discussed this with him?" Savannah asked.

Bridgette shook her head in response.

"I will, though. I just wanted to talk it over with you first. There wouldn't be a point in saying anything to him unless you agreed. So, what do you say?"

"Like I said, I want a baby. More than anything in this world, but it's a lot to consider and think about. I can't just say yes without at least thinking everything through. Plus, I'd have to talk to Julius about it first," said Savannah, poking at a cherry tomato in her salad with her fork. "It'll affect the both of us. And I suggest you do the same with Nick."

"I will, but only after you give me your decision," said Bridgette, taking a sip of her lemonade. "I really hope that you'll seriously consider it, Savannah. At least in the next few days since your surgery is coming up soon, and we'd need to go through the process of retrieving your eggs with the doctor's consent, of course."

Savannah looked at her sister and couldn't help but to shake her head in amusement. It shouldn't have been much of a surprise to her that Bridgette would offer to do something like this. It was the hallmark of who she was. She had definitely given her that sense of hope back she'd lost when Dr. Pennington had uttered those awful two words. Even if she decided not to go through with it, she'd always be grateful to her big sister for giving her that.

Chapter Eleven

S avannah was happier than she had been over the past few weeks and she had her big sister to thank for that. She couldn't wait to tell Julius about the wonderful blessing that Bridgette had offered them. It had been a few hours since Bridgette had left, and Savannah mulled over the pros and cons, especially after doing some research of her own. The whole in vitro fertilization process wouldn't be easy, and seemed quite taxing with the hormone injections to produce multiple eggs and then, the actual egg retrieval procedure, which sounded painful enough. She couldn't help to think if she'd be putting too much stress on her body, considering her upcoming surgery or if it would affect the cancer in any way. She didn't want to make a bad situation worse. And then, there were the costs.

Basically, it would be a small fortune just for one IVF cycle, and she would have to find out how much if any that her medical insurance would cover. Her surgery and treatment would already be costly even with her insurance. She and Julius wasn't hurting for money in the least bit with his thriving law practice combined with her handsome salary, but their lavish wedding and seven-day honeymoon in Bora

Bora had set them back a little financially, so Julius was more conscious about their spending habits. And there was one more thing that had popped up in her mind that she hated to keep thinking about, but it had been a nagging thought that plagued her since she learned of the cancer—her mortality.

What if once she went through the entire process of surgery, chemotherapy and radiation the cancer came back and somewhere more vital to her life like her lungs? She could die and leave her child motherless, which was a dismal thought. All of the tests she'd undergone during her appointment with Dr. Stein hadn't shown any signs of that right now, but they were going to remove some of her lymph nodes during her surgery to make sure, but long term, there was no guarantee. While all of those thoughts ran through her mind, it didn't quell her maternal urge. Now that it had been sparked again, she wouldn't be able to contain it. She had another chance at motherhood, and she couldn't think of a more perfect person to ensure that would happen.

Bridgette was a great mother to her nephews, and Savannah only hoped she could mirror that with her own child. Bridgette had practically raised her and Ivy being the oldest, and even though she still thought of them as her baby sisters, and was sometimes overprotective, Savannah knew it was only because she felt a certain responsibility for them. She just wished that Ivy realized that as well. She hated seeing her and Bridgette fighting with each other all the time and it disheartened her. She really missed the closeness they shared and she prayed that they could get it back. Life was such a short journey and having to face her own mortality made it a glaring reality.

Savannah still felt uneasy about the unknown, but right now, she didn't want to think about that. She wanted to focus on the positive, which is why she'd texted Julius earlier, after deciding that she wanted to take Bridgette up on her offer. She wanted him to meet her at one of their favorite restaurants, Morton's Steakhouse for a nice dinner out when he left work, and fortunately he'd be able to, which she considered another blessing she'd received that day. It was what they needed since they'd been so disconnected.

Savannah knew that lately, she hadn't been acting like the wife he deserved, and she truly felt bad about that because he'd done nothing but be supportive, no matter how much she had tried to push him away. She wanted them to get back to being the happy newlyweds that they had been before they'd walked into Dr. Pennington's office a few weeks ago, only to have everything they'd planned for their new married life together, take a turn for the worst. At least as much as they could be with what was looming ahead of them, but she had to give those worries to God, as her mother would often say.

It would be their first evening out since everything transpired and Savannah was looking forward to it. She'd always enjoyed their date nights because they'd started waning with Julius working all of the time. It felt like forever since she'd gotten dressed in anything other than pajamas.

This is going to be a great night, she thought as she gave herself a once over in the full length mirror in their bedroom, smiling at her reflection and for the first time, truly feeling like everything would be okay. She stood there for a moment studying her round face that she'd lightly applied make-up to. She knew Ivy would approve of how well she'd "beat her face", as she liked to call it. The soft pink lipstick she'd chosen, accentuated her chocolate complexion with just the right amount of foundation. It was quite a transformation from the frumpy, disheveled look she'd been sporting.

"I hope Julius likes this dress," she said.

Savannah turned at different angles, approving of how the black, floral-print maxi dress flowing down past her ankles fit her petite, but curvy frame. She ran her fingers through her soft, dark brown hair, wisps of curls falling on her shoulders and began to wonder how much she would change physically when she had to undergo treatment. Would she lose a tremendous amount of weight? Would her hair fall out in patches or would she end up completely bald? Would she turn into a shell of the woman staring back at her in the mirror's reflection? As much as she wanted to push those thoughts out of her mind, she couldn't, and she wasn't a vain woman at all. It was just so scary to think about. Savannah had witnessed her father's demise from cancer, so she couldn't help but wonder if she would suffer the same fate.

"Stop this," she said, scolding herself. "This too shall pass."

She felt those familiar emotions that had plagued her over the past few weeks and willed herself once again to focus on the positive. She was blessed with a support system that she knew many in her situation didn't have, so she had a lot to be grateful for. She smiled as she thought about being a mother and she felt herself begin to well up, but she refused to cry, especially since she'd taken care to put on make-up. She couldn't help the joy she felt, and she prayed that Julius would be just as happy about Bridgette's offer as she was because while she wanted this almost more than life itself, it wouldn't be worth it if he wasn't on board with it. As her husband, she had to respect whatever opinion he might have about it whether good or bad, but she was hoping for the former.

Chapter Twelve

Savannah could hardly contain her excitement as she and Julius ate their steak dinners and shared a bottle of red wine. She'd missed these intimate moments, and seeing how relaxed and content he was, she felt it was the right time to tell him the good news.

"Babe, I know we've been dealing with a lot lately and it's not something that either of us would've imagined we'd be going through, and I feel like I should apologize for that."

He frowned. "For what?"

"I don't want to be a burden. You didn't sign up for this," said Savannah, gazing at him.

"I would never think that, sweetheart. This isn't something for you to blame yourself about. It's a setback, but we'll overcome it. And I want you to start affirming that as well. Staying positive is half of the battle."

Savannah smiled. "Well, I have some news that could help with that."

"It has to be pretty good because your face is lit with excitement. And anything that can put that beautiful smile on my wife's face excites me as well. I've missed seeing you smile," he mused.

Savannah felt a twinge of sadness because she knew how hard it had been for him to witness her withdraw into a depression, but hopefully, this news would make up for it.

"You know when we met with Dr. Stein and he discussed with us our possible options for fertility?"

Julius took a sip of his cabernet sauvignon and nodded. "I do. Well, somewhat. If I'm being honest, I was more concerned with your overall health. That was all I was focused on at that moment. So, I really only heard bits and pieces."

Savannah knew that to be true because he'd kicked right into attorney mode, firing off questions at Dr. Stein quicker than the older man could answer them. Savannah was speechless, so she wasn't equipped mentally to ask anything or hear any more bad news. She was on the verge of a breakdown then.

"He mentioned freezing my eggs and having them stored to have them implanted later if it was something we wanted to consider."

Julius chewed a piece of his medium rare steak and washed it down with wine before he responded.

"Now that, I remember. And I have to say; I thought it was kind of off-the-wall, considering they'd have to be implanted into someone else for obvious reasons. And there's no way I would do something so creepy."

Savannah didn't like the sound of that at all.

"Why do you think it's creepy?" she asked.

"I guess seeing another woman pregnant with my child other than my wife would be jarring. I just don't know if I could do it, especially with a total stranger."

Savannah didn't want to get deterred by his words, but she was starting to feel defeated before she could even tell him. She was hoping that he'd see things differently once she did.

"But, what if we knew the person? Someone close to us?" she asked, her eyes searching his for any sign that he'd be willing to consider it, but she saw nothing. In fact, he looked repulsed by the notion. Then, he gave her a questioning look.

"What is it that you have to tell me, sweetheart because—,"

"Bridgette offered to be our surrogate," she blurted out, cutting him off.

Savannah couldn't discern the look displayed on his face as he peered at her over the wine glass at his lips. His brows were slightly furrowed and it seemed as if he was trying to decide whether to take a sip of his wine or down the entire glass in one swift gulp. He didn't do either as he placed the glass back down on the table.

"Isn't that great news, honey?" Savannah asked. Her voice filled with joy despite the uncertainty she felt about how their conversation would end.

"Wow," Julius responded.

"That's what my initial reaction was as well. I really didn't know how I felt about it, but after mulling it over afterwards, I think it's a great idea," Savannah exclaimed.

Julius leaned back into the booth they were seated in next to each other. He looked as if he was at a loss for the right words to say.

"I know it's a bit overwhelming to think about, and I really do understand your reservations, but this is good news for us, honey. We can have the baby we've been talking about pretty much since we've been together. And Bridgette wants to give us that."

"That's quite a sacrifice for her to be willing to make, I must say. She already has a lot going on. Do you think it's a good idea for her to try and have a baby for us as well? It seems like a bit much," Julius said. "And more importantly, how does Nick feel about all of this?"

"She was going to talk with him about it after she received our blessing."

Julius frowned.

"I don't like the sound of that, Savannah. I mean, don't you think she should've discussed the idea with him first before presenting you with it? As her husband, he should know something like that. It would affect both of them. Not to mention the boys."

"I understand that and I told her that, but you know how Bridgette is. She's very strong-willed about something she's passionate about. But, I'm sure she will."

Julius still didn't look like he was convinced. "While I'm grateful that Bridgette would like to do this, I'm just not so sure about it, baby. There is a lot to consider here. And furthermore, I don't want it to cause any problems in their marriage."

Savannah was beginning to feel discouraged because it was sounding like Julius wasn't going to consent and she would be devastated.

"What about our marriage? This is something we've both wanted and I'm afraid of what will happen to us by not being able to have any children," Savannah said, feeling herself getting emotional.

Julius grabbed her hand. "While I know that we've always talked about having a family, that's not why I married you. I'd be lying if I said I wouldn't be a little disappointed, but if there's a choice regarding your health and versus having a child, I'm going to choose you without question. My love for you is unconditional and I hope you realize that. And, there are always other options we could look into."

"I feel the same, honey. And thank you for saying that because to be honest, I've been worried about that," she said, ignoring the last part of his comment. She knew he was referring to adoption, and it's not like it was something she hadn't thought about, but it wasn't what she wanted to do. It probably seemed selfish, but she wanted a child with her husband—a biological child.

"These past few weeks have been really traumatic for me, and I'm thankful that you've been there for me even when I was acting like a spoiled brat. I think I fell in love with you all over again," Savannah smiled at him and he leaned in and placed a kiss on her lips. Savannah wanted to do something she hadn't felt like doing since her diagnosis, and that was make love to her husband, which she planned on doing when they got home. After her surgery, it would be awhile before they would be able to, so she needed to take advantage of it while she still could.

"Will you at least consider Bridgette's offer? I know you have concerns and believe me, I did too, but I really want this for us, honey. Can you imagine holding our very own child when it's all over?" Savannah asked, getting back on topic.

"I have to admit, that would be pretty awesome, wouldn't it?" Julius said, smiling and Savannah felt like he was starting to consider it.

"Yes, honey. And we could even end up with multiple babies at once since that happens quite often with in vitro fertilization. Now, that would be awesome."

"Maybe for us, but I don't know how Bridgette would feel about having to do that again. She seemed like she was struggling at the end of her pregnancy with the boys."

"She loved being pregnant with the twins." Savannah chuckled and so did Julius.

"Oh gosh," Julius exclaimed, shaking his head with a disgusted look on his face.

Savannah frowned. "What is it, honey?"

"I just thought about the fact that she'd have to actually go through delivery. I love Bridgette, but I have no interest at all in seeing her womanly parts," Julius announced and Savannah burst out laughing.

She laughed so hard she had tears coming from her eyes. Julius laughed along with her, and Savannah was happy that they were finding their light again after the past few weeks of darkness.

Chapter Thirteen

Back in Atlanta, after spending two weeks in Los Angeles working on the set of an upcoming TV show, Ivy was exhausted. She caught the earliest flight she could find out of LAX airport and once she'd gotten back to her townhouse nestled in the beautiful community of Buckhead, she parked her luggage at the front door in the foyer, peeling her clothes off along the way to the master bathroom for a hot shower; her ritual after a long flight. And afterwards, she put her iPhone on Do Not Disturb mode, crawled into bed and slept most of the day.

She could've probably slept another few hours, but the constant rumbling in her stomach wouldn't let her and she didn't have any food in the house and even worse—no wine, so she'd had to make a run to Publix. Now back home, she'd popped open her favorite brand of red wine, filled her wineglass to the rim, warmed up some soup, and made herself a sandwich to go along with it. It was times like these when she longed to be home in Charlotte with her sisters.

It was Sunday, so they'd be enjoying a hearty dinner at one of their houses after attending church together. Bridgette usually cooked the majority of the meal with Ivy and Savannah contributing something store bought, and Bridgette making a quip about their non-cooking skills. Afterwards, they'd enjoy whatever dessert Bridgette baked while watching one of their favorite movies. It was their sister time and Ivy always looked forward to it because now that Bridgette's bakery was steadily growing in its popularity and Savannah was a newlywed and Ivy traveling even more, their time together was almost becoming a rarity. She really missed her sisters.

Ivy hadn't spoken to Bridgette since her last visit home during Easter weekend other than sending her a few text messages when she hadn't been able to reach Savannah. When they'd all gotten together that Saturday at Savannah's house for the Easter egg hunt and barbecue, Bridgette still acted as if she had an attitude with Ivy, so she'd kept her distance. Ivy wanted to keep the mood peaceful, especially for Savannah's sake. She could tell she was in turmoil emotionally, though she was trying to be strong and Bridgette was glued to her side. Ivy had thought she was being a bit overbearing, but she kept quiet and reserved her opinions to herself. It was the same when they all reconvened for Easter dinner that Sunday. Ivy ended up leaving right after, making an excuse that she had an early flight back to Atlanta that next day when she wasn't leaving until Tuesday morning. She was saddened that their weekend together had been overcast by traumatic news and bickering. It had been too much.

When she'd texted Bridgette inquiring about Savannah because she hadn't been able to reach her, she'd respond with short, curt messages sometimes hours later and a few times, not at all. Ivy would shake her head in irritation at her older sister's behavior because she really didn't understand it. Bridgette acted as if Ivy had done something personal to her, and it didn't make any sense, but that was how she behaved sometimes and Ivy had decided that she wasn't going to worry about it. She hadn't had much time to anyway with her work schedule.

Ivy had just sat down to eat when her iPhone chimed. She looked at the screen and saw a text message from Kean. She hadn't spoken to him much either over the past few weeks, but he always seemed to know when she was back in Atlanta.

Be back in the ATL tomorrow. Early flight out of Philly. Still owe you a nice dinner. Any plans tomorrow night?

Nope. All yours… She replied.

Hmmm…I like the sound of that.

I'll bet you do. Ivy typed.

LOL! You set yourself up for that one, he responded.

Ivy laughed because she could picture the devious smirk he was known to wear on his face when joking around with her. She was looking forward to seeing him, but she wouldn't admit that to him. She loved the thrill of being courted. Women were too eager these days to sleep with men, instead of taking the time to learn if they were right for each other.

Get your mind out of my panties, Ivy replied.

Their playful text banter went on a few more minutes before they agreed on a time to get together the following day.

After finishing the remains of her light meal, she decided to call Savannah and check up on her. Ivy was surprised by the upbeat tone in her voice when she answered.

"Good evening, Bubbling Brown Sugar." Ivy quipped. "Sounds like you're doing much better."

"Yes, Ivy League. Much better, thanks to our sister."

Ivy paused at the mention of Bridgette's name.

"What has she done now?"

Savannah chuckled. "Are you sitting down?" she asked.

"Yeah. Why? What's going on?" Ivy's voice was filled with apprehension.

"The more important question I should ask is do you have a glass of wine because you might need it after I share this news with you," said Savannah.

Ivy could hear the excitement in her voice; so she knew it couldn't be anything else bad. "As a matter of fact, I do. So spill it. What's up?"

Savannah laughed and it sounded good to hear her in better spirits after the few tough weeks she'd had. Ivy didn't know what Bridgette had done to get her there, but she couldn't wait to find out. She heard Savannah inhale a deep breath and then exhale.

"Bridgette's going to carry my baby," Savannah blurted out.

"I beg your pardon?" Ivy asked. Her brows were furrowed in confusion. Now, she knew she hadn't been in the family loop and she'd only spoken to Savannah maybe twice since her last visit home, but what she was telling her wasn't making much sense.

"Bridgette offered to be my surrogate. I'm going to have my eggs removed and then we're going to have them fertilized with Julius's sperm and then implant them into Bridgette." Savannah announced this news as if she was talking about changing her hair color.

Ivy was stunned. She couldn't form the words to respond.

"Ivy, did you hear what I said?" Savannah demanded after a few seconds of silence had passed.

"Yes, but I don't know if I really heard you correctly," Ivy murmured.

"I said—," Savannah began, but Ivy cut her off.

"Savannah, you don't have to repeat it."

Ivy reached for the bottle of merlot in front of her and refilled her glass. Savannah was right in her discernment that she'd need it. In fact, she'd probably have to open another bottle.

"What's wrong, Ivy? I thought you'd be happy. I'll have the baby I wanted now thanks to our sister," said Savannah, her voice filled with disappointment.

"Nothing's wrong, sis. I am happy for you, but I'm just a little surprised. That's all." Ivy took a long swig from her wineglass. "It's not every day that you hear this kind of news, especially in a black family."

"What does being black have to do with anything?" Savannah's tone was defensive.

"I'm just saying. I've never heard of black people doing this, and certainly not anybody that we know. It seems a bit strange."

And in Ivy's opinion, it was real strange. She'd worked with a few celebrities, mainly white women who'd paid other women to carry their babies, but that was the wacky part of the entertainment business and she didn't know them personally, so it didn't affect her.

"Strange for whom? We're sisters. Not strangers," said Savannah.

"Savannah, I don't want you to take what I'm saying the wrong way, and I sense that's what's happening and that's not my intent. I'm just trying to understand."

"What's for you to understand? I thought that my dreams of starting a family with Julius were over, but now, I have the chance to see it come into fruition. Thanks to Bridgette," said Savannah.

Ivy couldn't help but to roll her eyes at the mention of her oldest sister. She hadn't talked to her in a while, but as soon as she hung up with Savannah, Bridgette would be getting a call from her whether she answered or not. And Ivy already knew their conversation wouldn't be pleasant after she gave her opinion on this surrogacy foolishness.

"Like I said before, Savannah. I'm happy for you because I know how much you've wanted this, but I have some concerns and I'd be remiss if I didn't voice them. And, I have to be honest here, I don't know if this is a good idea," said Ivy.

"Why not?" Savannah asked and Ivy could hear the irritation in her voice.

Ivy took another sip from her wineglass, inhaled a deep breath and released it before answering her sister. She didn't want to hurt Savannah's feelings and quell her joy. She knew how depressed she'd been and if this was what was getting her back to happy, then she didn't want to interfere with that, especially with the battle she'd have to endure to rid her body of cancer, which Ivy was more concerned with.

"I think your focus should be on getting better, Savannah. We've all been through this cancer thing before with Daddy, so you know the toll it's going to take on you physically and emotionally. I think you'll be adding unnecessary stress."

"I appreciate your concern, Ivy, but if anything, it'll help me get through everything I'll have to go through, knowing that a rainbow in the form of this baby will be something I can look forward to at the end of this storm. You'll see," said Savannah with assurance.

Ivy didn't want to keep pressing her opinion on her sister, so she refrained for now, at least where Savannah was concerned.

"I guess I will," said Ivy, now mulled in her thoughts. She half-listened as Savannah talked with excitement about motherhood. Ivy wondered if her and Bridgette had talked it over with Julius and Nick and how they'd felt about all of this, but she remained silent. Again, it all felt so strange.

Chapter Fourteen

B ridgette had gotten her boys off to bed and now she was in her bedroom waiting on Nick to come out of the shower so she could finally talk with him. She knew she'd receive some resistance, but she was ready for it. She was feeling hopeful and thought back to her conversation a few hours ago with Savannah.

"We want to do it," said Savannah, when Bridgette answered her call. She'd just gotten home from church and was changing out of the dress she'd worn into more comfortable attire so she could start dinner. She'd been home alone since Nick had taken the boys out for a movie they'd been excited about seeing.

"Oh Savannah. That makes me so happy. I didn't really know if you would, but I'm glad you made this decision. So, I take it Julius gave you his blessing?"

"Yes, after much skepticism, but he wants a baby as much as I do, so that outweighed everything else. He just wants to make sure the process won't interfere with my treatment. That's his main concern."

"Of course. Mine too. We won't do anything until we have full consent from the doctors." Bridgette said, as she removed her diamond stud earrings and stored them in her jewelry box sitting on her dresser.

"I'm going to give Dr. Stein a call in the morning and get a referral for a fertility specialist. And then, we'll go from there," said Savannah. *"Have you talked to Nick yet?"*

"No, but I'm going to tonight. Now, that I have your blessing."

"How do you think he's going to react?" Savannah asked.

"I don't know, but I'm hoping he'll be open to it."

"I'll be praying because I'm really excited about this, and it's all I've been thinking about. And Bridgette, I'm so grateful that you want to do this for us. There are not enough words in the English language to tell you how much. Thank you so much, big sissy. I love you so much," said Savannah and Bridgette could hear her welling up and it caused her to also.

"I love you too, baby sis. You're going to be a great Mommy and I can't wait to experience it with you," Bridgette said, wiping a tear that had fallen down her cheek.

She blinked back tears, thinking about the conversation with her sister, as she sat up in bed with pillows propped behind her, flipping through the latest issue of *Essence* magazine, ironically with singer Kelly Rowland cradling her new baby on the cover, their Mother's Day issue—reaffirming her decision. In her opinion, every woman should be able to experience the maternal glow that Kelly was displaying, especially if they had the desire like Savannah. Bridgette loved being pregnant with her boys, and while Savannah wouldn't be able to experience that part of it, Bridgette hoped that the end result would make up for it.

Bridgette's iPhone buzzed on the nightstand with Ivy's image and name displayed on the screen. She let it go to voicemail. Ivy had sent her a text message earlier that said: *We need to talk.* Bridgette hadn't responded then either. She didn't have too much to say to her right now anyway. But, their baby sister was going through a tough time and Bridgette thought Ivy would've made more of an effort to be present for her, but she hadn't and it was typical. Ivy only thought about Ivy and Bridgette was sick of her selfishness. She was two seconds from really letting her have it. So, it was best that they kept their distance. And, she certainly didn't have the energy to deal with her now. She had far more pressing matters to concern herself with at the present.

A few minutes later, Nick emerged from their master bathroom. He was naked and still damp with beads of moisture from his shower. Bridgette looked up from her magazine, her eyes following his milk chocolate, athletic frame as he strolled the distance to their large, walk-in closet. After ten years of marriage, seeing her husband nude still elevated her body temperature.

Nick had been a champion swimmer all through high school, which earned him a full athletic scholarship at North Carolina State University where they'd met over two decades ago as freshmen. Now a high school swim coach, he tried to be a role model for his students in taking care of his body and staying active, working out at least three times a week and for the most part, watching what he ate. At forty years old, his body hadn't changed much. Bridgette wished she could say the same about hers, but the twins could be blamed for that.

When Nick returned from the closet wearing a pair of boxers and settled in next to her in bed with the remote control in his hand, no doubt to turn to ESPN to look at sports highlights, Bridgette decided that she wasn't going to waste any more time and while she still had the nerve, she'd get straight to it before he got too comfortable.

"Honey, I'd like to talk to you about something," Bridgette said, staring at Nick's profile. His attention was focused on the large flat screen TV and the two sportscasters talking.

"What's that?"

"Well, I'd like to help Savannah and Julius with something, but I want to see what you think about it."

"Okay? What's that?"

Bridgette could hear the tone of his voice change slightly with uncertainty about what she was going to say, and she took a deep breath.

"I'm hoping you'll keep an open mind about it."

That comment gave her his full attention because now he was peering at her. Bridgette averted her eyes toward the TV.

"Bridgette? What's going on?" Nick asked.

Bridgette heard impatience in his voice. "I offered Savannah a solution to having a baby. Nick, she deserves it. So does Julius," Bridgette declared, her voice going up an octave. She hadn't even told him what it was yet, but she already felt the need to defend herself.

Nick remained silent, but she could tell from the look on his face that he wasn't going to like what she had to say next, so she braced herself for his reaction.

"I offered to carry a baby for her," Bridgette said. "I want to be her surrogate."

His response was slow because she assumed he was trying to process what she'd just said.

"You're kidding? Right?" Nick replied dryly. His voice was devoid of emotion.

"I've never been more serious about anything in my life."

Nick stared at her like she'd grown an extra eye in the middle of her forehead. "Are you having a moment of temporary insanity, woman?" he asked her with seriousness. "Because I know good and doggone well you ain't saying what I think you are."

"You heard me right, Nick. I want to carry a baby for my sister. But most importantly, I want your support."

Nick guffawed and Bridgette glared at him. There was nothing funny about this topic at all, so she didn't appreciate him laughing about it, even if he was being facetious.

"Bridgette, have you lost your mind? There's no way in the history of life that I would ever co-sign on something so foolish. You've been watching too much Lifetime," he retorted, shaking his head as if what she'd said was the most ridiculous thing he'd ever heard and refocusing his attention on the TV, making Bridgette feel as if he was dismissing her.

"Nick, I want to do it. I'm going to do it," Bridgette countered with finality.

He looked back at her with a deep frown on his face. "I've let you pretty much run things how you want to in this marriage without much interference and against my better judgment at times, but I'm still the man of this house and as long as I am, you won't be doing this. I forbid it."

Now, it was Bridgette's turn to frown.

"Nicholas Langston Harper, you can't forbid me to do anything. We're not in the Fifties."

"If it affects the welfare of this family, I most certainly will. Have you even thought about those boys sleeping down the hall? What do you plan on telling them when you're walking around here with a swollen belly they think has their brother or sister inside of it, but in actuality it's their cousin? It's ludicrous, Bridgette. There's no other way of putting it."

Nick shook his head like the thought of it all disgusted him.

"If we explain to them the situation, they'll understand it, Nick. They're smart young men for their age," Bridgette argued.

"They're eight. Nowhere near men," Nick countered. "And speaking of age, you're no spring chicken yourself."

"Meaning?" Bridgette asked, folding her arms across her chest and glaring at him.

"I'm not a doctor or anything, but I know you're much older than you were when you were pregnant with the boys. It could be dangerous."

"Forty is hardly old. Women my age and older have babies everyday. And yes, there are some risks for women after a certain age, but that's with any pregnancy."

"But why would you even chance it, Bridgette? Now, I know that you love your sister. I do too. And I'm sympathetic to what her and Julius are going through. I truly am. But, you have to think about our family."

"I am. We're all family, Nick. We should all be able to help each other if we can."

"Within reason. And this, my dear, isn't reasonable at all. Have you thought about the what ifs? God forbid it, but what if something happens to Savannah as a result of the cancer and then we're stuck with another child that we both agreed a long time ago that we weren't going to have."

"I didn't agree on anything. I just went along with what you wanted. But, I've always wanted more children," Bridgette said, now, fighting back tears.

This conversation was becoming far more emotionally draining than she had anticipated, and she was ready to end it. She'd made up her mind, and she wasn't going to change it. Nick would just have to understand because it was her body and she had a right to make decisions regarding it. And plus, she'd already told Savannah she was going to do it, and she certainly wasn't going to renege on that and risk sending her sister back into a depression.

"Well, that's certainly news to me, but that's neither here nor there. I think I've made my stance on this whole surrogate tomfoolery quite clear, so I'm done talking about it," Nick declared, looking back at the TV and dismissing Bridgette a second time. But, it was one time too many for her.

Bridgette swung her legs to the side of the bed and planted her bare feet on the cool hardwood floor below her.

"Where are you going?"

"This tomfool is going to sleep in the guest room," Bridgette announced, her back facing him as she stood. She snatched her magazine from the bed and her iPhone off the nightstand so she could set her alarm on it to get up in the morning since she wouldn't be using the alarm clock in their bedroom. It would be the first time in ten years of them being married that they slept apart while being in the same house. But as the saying went, there's a first time for everything.

"Well, if that's what you feel like you have to do. But while you're in there, I suggest you think more about how your decisions are going to affect us all. I know you have a problem doing that, but make sure you *really* think about all of the risks."

Bridgette didn't bother to look at him or respond as she marched out of their bedroom, but his last sentence made her uneasy and she wondered what he really wanted to say. Was he threatening to leave her if she went through with this? He would never do that. Would he?

Chapter Fifteen

"Put me down," Ivy demanded through her laughter. Kean had her lifted over his shoulder with her rear end in the air.

"Not until you call me Big Papa," said Kean.

"I ain't calling you Big anything. Now, put me down. I got to pee from all that wine I drank."

"Well, you better get to talking then," said Kean, smacking her on the buttocks.

"I'm serious, Kean. I really have to go, so I suggest you put me down or I won't be responsible if there's an accident right on this nice, expensive shirt you're wearing," Ivy warned, her laughter turning into giggles. She did have one too many glasses of merlot during dinner.

Kean surrendered and gently placed Ivy on her feet. He slapped her on the behind a second time as she raced out of the living room. His laughter filled her ears.

"Hurry up so you can give me my foot massage," Kean called after her.

"Boy, bye. I'm not touching your rusty feet with my freshly manicured hands," Ivy yelled over her shoulder.

"That was the deal. You can't renege," Kean yelled back.

Minutes later, Ivy returned to the living room and joined Kean on the couch, stretching her legs across his lap. She wiggled her cotton candy-pink colored toes.

"My feet could use massaging, though," Ivy said with a sheepish grin. She leaned back on the arm of the sofa to get more comfortable.

"Not until I get mine first. A deal is a deal," said Kean as he turned his body to hers, stretching his long and lean legs across hers. He had a wide grin spread across his face.

Ivy always thought his best feature was his teeth other than his dark chocolate complexion, which she likened to Godiva chocolate, another indulgence of hers other than red wine. Kean had the pearliest, whitest teeth Ivy had ever seen on a man, which reminded her of Tic Tac candy mints. She thought he favored another famous athlete and her favorite quarterback of all-time, Michael Vick, except Kean was much taller.

"You lost fair and square, babes, so it's time to pay the piper," he added. Ivy rolled her eyes playfully. She'd lost in a game of Monopoly.

"Everything is a competition with you. Isn't it?" Ivy replied.

"I'm a natural bred athlete so I get it honest. Now, get to rubbing. I ain't got all night."

Ivy grabbed an accent pillow from behind her and threw it at him. He dodged it with his forearm and laughed, pulling her into him and tickling her. Ivy's laughter filled the room as she wiggled to get out of his reach.

"Stop it, Kean. I'll give you your massage," Ivy conceded.

"That's what I thought," he retorted.

A few minutes later, Kean rested his head back on the arm of the sofa with his eyes closed as Ivy kneaded the soles of his feet with her fingers.

"Girl, you got skills," he said. "Now, if I could get you to use those skills in the kitchen."

Ivy sucked her teeth.

"Says the man with the personal chef."

He chuckled. "I still need a woman to cook for me sometimes and a frozen Stouffer's lasagna in the oven ain't it," Kean joked.

"Well, I didn't hear you complaining when you were wolfing it down," Ivy responded and Kean laughed.

"I have to admit that I was a little surprised by your invitation to dinner. I thought you enjoyed being wined and dined."

"Of course. It's a nice thing every now and then, but I'd much rather be in the comfort of my own home. I don't get to enjoy it often," said Ivy.

"I get it. It's hard being away from your loved ones and having to travel so much. That's why any chance I get, I make it a point to come home and spend time with them, especially with my baby girl. She's growing up so fast and I'm afraid that I'll miss something."

"You sound like a different person when you talk about her. You light up. Reminds me of my dad. He loved his daughters like no other." Ivy smiled at the thought of her father and sisters, but she felt an overwhelming sense of sadness. She missed them all, especially her sisters. It almost felt like they were estranged and Ivy didn't like that feeling. Bridgette still hadn't returned her any of her messages from the day before, so either she was busy or ignoring her and she was leaning toward the latter, and that hurt her feelings.

"Most definitely. Marley is my world. I can honestly say she changed me for the better. Now, don't get it twisted. I'm still a work in progress, but I tend to think things through instead of acting on impulse."

Ivy smiled in response. She was glad that he was comfortable enough around her to show that side of himself. It was refreshing.

Kean hadn't had the best reputation when they'd first met, but Ivy had always been one to form her own opinions about people, and so far, he hadn't lived up to that bad boy, womanizer image that preceded him and was synonymous with male athletes. And she'd dated a few.

"Sounds like a special little girl," Ivy said.

"She definitely is. She reminds me a lot of you," he said. His light brown eyes bore into hers.

"How so?" Ivy queried.

"Stubborn," Kean replied with a smirk.

Ivy rolled her eyes. "Whatever," she retorted, pushing his long limbs from atop of hers.

"Hold up. You didn't massage my other foot." He laughed.

She picked up another pillow and tossed it at him, hitting him in the face. His laughter was infectious and Ivy laughed along with him. She really enjoyed his company and he seemed to feel the same. He was a nice distraction from her thoughts about her sisters.

"I'd really like you to meet Marley, Ivy. I think y'all would hit it off," Kean said.

Ivy didn't know about that one. She didn't actually consider herself to be kid-friendly. Now, she loved her nephews, Dylan and Ryan without question, but she didn't have to interact with them on a daily basis either.

"We'll see," was all she said. She was uncomfortable with the topic of meeting his daughter, and she wanted to talk about something else. It was still fairly early, but the three glasses of wine she'd consumed at dinner were starting to catch up to her. Plus, she was still a bit jet lagged. But, if she was honest with herself, she wasn't ready for their evening together to end just yet.

"You feel like watching a movie?" she asked. "It's Monday night, so there's not much on TV. Well, unless you're into watching ratchet TV like *Love and Hip Hop*?"

"Nah. I'm good on that. We can do a movie, though. As long as it ain't one of those male-bashing, Tyler Perry movies I'm cool with whatever you want to watch," said Kean, chuckling.

She laughed. "Hater. I love his movies, but I'm biased. My first big gig was on the set of *Why Did I Get Married?* I did Jill Scott's make-up."

"Jilly from Philly. That's my girl. I've met her at a few events in Philadelphia. I'm a big fan of her music. Her acting, not so much," said Kean.

Ivy chuckled, shaking her head. "I love her new album. It's on heavy rotation. I play it daily."

"It is hot. I love that Track Fifteen. Jah-something other," said Kean.

"*Jah-ray-me-co-fas-ola*," Ivy sang. "That's my favorite too," she exclaimed.

"Wow, you have a beautiful voice," he complimented, causing Ivy to blush.

"Thank you," she said.

"Seems like you might've chosen the wrong profession."

Ivy shook her head.

"This voice is strictly for singing in the shower." They both laughed.

"I beg to differ. I hope I can hear more of it. I enjoyed it," he said, gazing at her.

She didn't know if it was the effects of the wine or being in such close proximity to him, but she was feeling warm. Their chemistry was almost explosive. Ivy hadn't wanted to complicate things with sex because they were still in that friend zone, even though they'd shared kisses so intimate they might as well had. She knew he wasn't lacking in the sex department. He was a single, handsome, wealthy, professional athlete, and she'd be a fool to think he wasn't getting any, but he wasn't getting any of her goodies. Well, at least not yet anyway, which is why she needed to break the distance between them. If only momentarily.

Ivy stood to grab the remote to her Apple TV and pulled up the queue of movies she'd downloaded, but hadn't had a chance to watch. The first movie on the list was *Addicted*, the popular book by author Zane that had been turned into a movie, featuring actress Sharon Leal who she'd also worked with on the set of *Why Did I Get Married?* and actor Boris Kodjoe. Ivy had been anticipating watching it, but she'd seen how steamy it was from the previews, and the lustful feelings she was having for Kean in that moment, there was no way she was going to watch that movie with him. So, she scrolled on to the next one, *Ride Along* with Kevin Hart and Ice Cube.

"What about this one?" she asked, joining him back on the sofa.

"Sure. Let's check it out. I hadn't seen it yet either," said Kean. "Anything Kevin Hart in is always funny." He wrapped his arms around her in a comfortable embrace with her head rested on his chest as the movie began to play.

"I feel like we're really booed up right now," Ivy joked.

"What's wrong with that? We could be boos. I'm ready when you are." He leaned in and placed a kiss on the top of her head. She couldn't help but blush at his gesture.

Ivy thought about what it would be like to be in a committed relationship with Kean from time to time, but it never moved her to want to actually be in one. It had been almost two years since her last—well, if you wanted to call it that, which still left an acidic taste in her mouth. And, she still had nightmares about it. No, she was definitely good on relationships because the last one almost killed her—literally.

Chapter Sixteen

Bridgette hadn't slept much the last two nights because she was still reeling from her argument with Nick about being Savannah's surrogate. Even though the queen-size bed in the guest room was comfortable enough, sleep just wouldn't come to her. She'd just lie there as hours passed. She was still too hurt and angry, and the thoughts racing through her mind wouldn't let her. Bridgette had hoped that Nick would come to her in the night and apologize for hurting her feelings and ask her back in their bed, but he hadn't. And this morning like the one prior, he'd practically ignored her when he'd come into the kitchen as she was making the boys their breakfast. There was no "good morning" or the kiss that usually followed. He just gave the boys their usual high fives, made his breakfast shake without so much as a glance at her and left the house to head to work.

Bridgette couldn't believe how he was acting, and even though she wanted to give him a piece of her mind, she refrained because her boys were present, but they were definitely going to revisit the situation later. She wouldn't be disrespected in her own home and she wasn't going to spend another night in the guest room either. They were going to have to come to some kind of resolution about this surrogacy issue because she wasn't going to back down. She was going to do it and that was that.

She could hardly keep her eyes open as she stared at the financial document she'd pulled up on her computer screen. She took a swig of her usual Starbucks java, hoping that it would give her the boost of energy she needed.

A few seconds later, the phone to her office rang and she frowned when she saw the name displayed on the caller ID. She ignored it until it stopped and then, it rang again. She blew out a deep breath before she picked up the receiver to try to calm her nerves that were already being worked on just by seeing who it was.

"What's up?" she asked, not bothering to hide her annoyance when she finally answered.

"Why have you been ignoring my calls?" asked the irate voice on the other end.

Bridgette rolled her eyes because she wasn't in the mood for Ivy's foolishness this morning, especially not after the night she'd had or morning for that matter.

"What is it, Ivy?"

"Why are you being so snappish, Bridgette? What is your problem?" Ivy demanded. Her voice sounding equally annoyed.

"I'm busy and I have a long day ahead of me, so I don't have time for your pettiness today," Bridgette retorted.

"Have you been busy every time I've called or texted you?"

Bridgette rolled her eyes again, but didn't respond.

"And who's being petty? You're the one who has been ignoring me. Not the other way around. And to be quite honest with you, I have no clue as to why. I just don't get it, but that's neither here nor there because that's not what I want to talk to you about," said Ivy.

"Well, I wish you would get to it because I have work to do," Bridgette snapped.

"This won't take long, so you'll be able to get back to icing your little cupcakes or whatever it is you do all day."

Bridgette was getting irritated with Ivy by the second. She'd insulted her again like it was nothing and she was two seconds from going off on her. She decided to ignore Ivy's little snide remark about what she did for a living, as if putting pounds of make-up on people's faces made what she did better. Ivy had really let her career go to her head and Bridgette was tired of it. Hobnobbing with the rich and famous and dating all of those athletes and actors had made Ivy more self-centered and arrogant than she already had been. That Hollywood ego had certainly rubbed off on her to the point where Bridgette couldn't stand to be around her sometimes. She'd become materialistic and in Bridgette's opinion, a borderline alcoholic with her voracious intake of red wine. She drank it like it was water. Although she loved her sister, she was disappointed in what she'd become and their parents would be disgusted much like she was.

"What is this I hear about you wanting to be Savannah's surrogate? And more importantly, why on God's green earth would you present such a ridiculous notion to her at such a vulnerable time in her life?" Ivy questioned.

"Because I can and I did. And really, it's none of your business, Ivy. And to answer your question, unlike you, I have sympathy for what Savannah is going through and whatever way I can help her to get through this, I'll do just that. So, I couldn't care less what you think about it quite frankly," Bridgette snapped and it was all she could do not to hang up on Ivy.

"Well, in my honest opinion, I think it's just another way for you to poke your nose into someone else's business. I could see if Savannah asked you to do this, but the fact of the matter is, she didn't. And furthermore, you should be more concerned with her concentrating on treatment and recovery and not giving her something else to stress over," Ivy stated.

"Well, you know what they say about opinions and again, this has nothing to do with you, Ivy. You're never here anyway which is typical; I thought that you would've made yourself a little more available knowing your sister is sick. But, I guess it's too much of a task to think about anyone else besides yourself."

Ivy snickered with sarcasm. "Savannah knows how much I love her and I don't have to justify it to you. But, just so you know, I will be there for her surgery and recovery. And I hope that whatever silly grudge you have against me, you'll put it to the side for her sake. She really doesn't need us bickering, especially over some foolishness. I won't go there with you. I refuse to. We can keep our distance as need be."

Bridgette rolled her eyes once again. "I certainly have no problem with that. Now, as I said, I have work to do. So, you have a nice day." She ended their call before Ivy could respond.

Their conversation had been pointless to say the least and it only irritated Bridgette further. Ivy had some nerve questioning her motives. It was almost like she'd forgotten the sacrifices Bridgette had made for her. She peered down at the scar on her left hand that extended the width of her thumb, a constant reminder of just how much.

Chapter Seventeen

A few hours later at home, Bridgette settled into the family room with her MacBook laptop when the boys went upstairs to their bedroom after having dinner. She'd decided to pick up a couple of pizzas because she was just too tired to cook after her day at the bakery, and partly to spite Nick since he always preferred a home cooked meal. She knew he would probably grumble about it when he got home from the gym, but just like he'd been ignoring her, she would reciprocate his behavior—two could play that game.

Bridgette was stretched out on her favorite red sectional creating a new seasonal menu for the bakery when her iPhone buzzed and Savannah's image appeared on the screen.

"Hey sis," Savannah said, when Bridgette answered.

"Hey, baby sis. What's going on with you?" Bridgette asked.

"I'm good. How are you? Was work really busy today?"

"Always, but I'm blessed that people still have a sweet tooth because that certainly keeps me in business. Did you have a chance to talk to Dr. Stein about your fertility decision?" Bridgette asked.

"I did. And he gave me a referral, but he recommended starting the in vitro fertilization process after my surgery. He doesn't see an issue with delaying chemo and radiation, but he'll only put it off for about eight to twelve weeks provided everything goes well with the surgery, so we'll basically be on the clock."

"Wow," said Bridgette.

"Julius is going to have Heather draw up a surrogacy contract. It turns out that she's handled these types of situations before since she practices family law, and she strongly suggests one, even though we're family and doing it on our own without the help of an agency. It's just to lay everything out in black and white." said Savannah.

"That sounds reasonable enough."

"And, she also mentioned that in her experience, along with the obvious medical screenings, psychological evaluations are usually recommended as well," said Savannah.

"I remember reading that, but I'm sure we'll be fine. I'm not one of those crazy women in those movies that'll kidnap the baby and try to keep it for myself," Bridgette joked, making Savannah giggle.

"What's the update on Nick? Is he budging any?" Savannah asked. "As your husband, he'd be required to go through all of the testing as well."

"He's still not speaking to me."

"Are you serious?" Savannah asked, and Bridgette could hear her disappointment.

"Well, probably because I told him I'm going to do it regardless. He'll just have to get over it."

"This is what I was afraid of. As much as I want this baby, I don't want it to be at the expense of your marriage, Bridgette. I would feel really guilty about that."

"Don't worry yourself about it, Savannah. I'll talk to him again and make him understand what a good thing this is. He'll come around," said Bridgette, even though she wasn't convinced of that herself. She was worried that he wouldn't.

"Are you sure because we don't have to do this?" asked Savannah. Bridgette knew it's not how she really felt.

"Nonsense. We're going to do it. So, go ahead and start setting up that nursery you've always talked about designing."

"Only if you'll go shopping with me. It'll be so much fun to baby shop together," said Savannah, and Bridgette could tell she was smiling. It shined through in her voice.

"I can't wait," said Bridgette, now smiling also.

"Okay. Well, I'll keep you posted on everything else once I meet with the fertility specialist and Heather draws up the contract. Do you still have the same attorney to be able to go over the contract once we get it?" Savannah asked.

"I do. I'll give her a call tomorrow and give her the heads up on what we're planning to do," said Bridgette.

"Sounds great. Oh, and by the way, I talked to your sister Sunday night and told her the news," Savannah said, chuckling.

Bridgette rolled her eyes like she'd been doing a lot lately when it pertained to Ivy.

"Ummph…well, unfortunately I had the displeasure as well. She really tried me today, and she didn't realize how close she came to really setting me off."

"Oh Lord. What is with you two these days? I don't understand what's going on and I wish one of you would clue me in," said Savannah.

"She called me to let know how much she disagreed with this whole thing regarding the surrogacy, and pretty much accused me of being a bad sister. And if that wasn't trifling enough, she insulted what I did for a living, almost like it was beneath what he does," Bridgette rebuffed.

"Wow. Are you kidding me?" Savannah exclaimed. "I could tell she wasn't feeling the idea, but I had no clue she'd call you and tell you so."

"No, but it's no surprise to me. That's how she behaves. Well, towards me anyway. I've really held my tongue about the things she's done and said, but just like she can't seem to do the same, I won't do it anymore either. Between her and Nick the past few days, I've really had my fill of them both."

"I really hate to hear this. But, like I told her when she was here last for Easter, I need you two to try and resolve whatever is going on because it's not that serious. We're sisters. And I don't want to sound so dismal, but life is much too short and our trio could end up a duo without warning. Just food for thought," said Savannah.

Bridgette didn't like the last part of her comment, and she hated for Savannah to be thinking in such a macabre manner.

"I hear you, and I do understand that. But, I won't continue to be disrespected, especially by people that are supposed to love me. I always have everybody else's best interest at heart, but it doesn't seem like anybody has mine. I'm really getting fed up with it," said Bridgette and she could feel herself getting riled up. The thought of both Ivy and Nick was making her angry.

"Just try and relax, sis. Because God is what?" she asked.

"Able," Bridgette answered.

"And He can do what?" Savannah asked.

"Turn any situation around," Bridgette responded, smiling now.

"Let the church say, 'Amen'.

"Amen," said Bridgette.

The two sisters shared a laugh, and Bridgette felt a little better, that is until she looked up and saw Nick staring at her from across the room.

"I've got to go, baby sis. Love you," Bridgette said before ending their call.

Chapter Eighteen

"**W**hat's up?" Bridgette asked, when Nick joined her on the sectional. He gazed at her a few seconds before responding.

"I just came back from meeting up with Jules," he said.

Bridgette didn't know how to respond, so she didn't. Since she had no idea that he and Julius were meeting, and Savannah certainly hadn't mentioned anything about it, so it was obvious she hadn't known either. But, Bridgette did have a pretty good idea what the topic of conversation was.

"Since you're dead set on doing this despite how I feel about it, then I guess the only thing left for me to say is that I won't stand in your way. I don't want to fight about this anymore," he continued.

"Nick, I absolutely care about your feelings, so please don't think that I—,"

He put up his hand to silence her.

"Let's not keep traveling down the same path. You've made your decision, so I guess that's that. And even though I don't agree with it, I understand it. You want your sister to have what we have. I get that. And, I think Jules deserves it as well. Heck, the way our boys love to be around him and how he treats them as if they're his own, I know he does."

Bridgette nodded in agreement.

"But, I will say that I hope in the future you'll think about all of these sacrifices you're always so quick to make for your sisters because I seriously doubt that if the roles were reversed they'd do the same."

Bridgette wanted to disagree with him, but decided to pick her battles. It didn't matter anyway because she never did the things she did for reciprocation. It was always out of love, and that's what family was about for her. Always had been and always would be.

"Honey, are you giving me your blessing or your resolve. There's a difference?" Bridgette asked.

"I don't think that matters now," he said, rising from his seat. "I'm going to turn in early tonight. I'm beat. But, you can join me later if you want to." He leaned down and placed a kiss on her forehead before leaving.

Bridgette was conflicted by his words. While she was happy that he'd finally done the right thing and invited her back in their bed, and he seemed to be semi on board with the surrogacy plan, she couldn't help but to feel that the issues regarding it weren't resolved, but she hoped that would change. What they were doing for Savannah and Julius was such a blessing, and Nick would see that in the end.

She picked up her iPhone and typed Savannah a message.

I don't know what your husband said to mine, but Operation Baby Yancey is a go!

Chapter Nineteen

Other than her wedding day, this had to be one of the happiest moments of her life. Savannah stared at the small monitor in awe of the two white, pea-sized images displayed on the screen of the ultrasound machine. She blinked back tears because her heart was so full of joy and gratitude in what she and her big sister were experiencing together.

"My babies," Savannah uttered at the sight of her embryos that had just been transferred into her sister's uterus. She gazed up at her husband, his face replete with just as much joy. Everything she'd endured over the past few months seemed worth it for what she felt in that moment. The nurse handed her a sonogram picture.

"Wow. I think they look like me already," Julius joked as he peered at the photo, causing everybody in the room to break out in laughter.

"Bridgette, how are you feeling, sis?" Savannah asked. She'd been holding her sister's hand during the transfer procedure as she lay on her back with her feet in stirrups and covered from the waist down.

"I feel fine. I can't believe we're finally doing this," said Bridgette, beaming as she stared at the screen. They were all donned in blue hairnets, gowns and booties.

"I know. If somebody would've told me a year ago that this would be our life, I would've thought they were crazy. The Lord really does work in mysterious ways," Savannah mused.

"He certainly works it out, but I had no doubt that He would," Bridgette said.

Savannah smiled in agreement.

"So, what's next Dr. Billingsley?" Savannah asked the fertility specialist.

"You'll go home and rest for the remainder of the day," Dr. Billingsley said to Bridgette as she removed her gloves and dropped them into a nearby trashcan. "Also, you'll continue your hormone injections for eight to ten weeks"—Bridgette groaned and the doctor chuckled, "but, I'll see you back here in about a week or so for a pregnancy test."

"Sounds good," said Bridgette.

"Thank you again, Dr. Billingsley," Savannah smiled at the attractive, forty-something-year-old, African-American woman.

"You're quite welcome. How have you been feeling since the retrieval?" she asked, referring to the egg retrieval procedure Savannah had five days ago, six weeks after her hysterectomy, which she'd had ironically, the Monday after Mother's Day. So, they'd been able to do a live transfer, instead of having her eggs frozen beforehand, but she would have the remaining embryos frozen since they'd all decided to transfer just two. She was praying for twins.

"I'm doing good as far as that's concerned. I start chemo and radiation next week. I'm a little nervous, but ready to get it started and over with."

"I understand, but you have a great team of doctors and I'm sure they will take good care of you," said Dr. Billingsley, removing Bridgette's feet from the stirrups.

"I have faith that they will."

"Mrs. Harper, I need you to lie here for an hour, and in the meantime, I'll gather your paperwork for check out. It was great to see you all again," said Dr. Billingsley; rising from the small stool she'd been sitting on.

They all thanked her again before she left the room with her nurse in tow.

"I'm going to duck out and make a call to the office," said Julius, placing a kiss on Savannah's cheek. She refrained from commenting on his need to conduct business since he had made the time to be there for she and Bridgette unlike Nick, who'd claimed he couldn't get off work.

"Good job, Bridge. You rock, girl," he said, causing Bridgette to giggle and then leaving the room.

"What a week this has been," said Savannah, sitting next to her sister on the small bed.

"I'd say, but we did it, sissy. And now, we wait for Baby Yancey—or more than one Baby Yancey," Bridgette joked, placing a hand on her stomach.

Savannah beamed at her sister's words. "I'm praying that they stick."

"It's already done. I can feel it," Bridgette exclaimed.

Savannah leaned her head on her sister's as she lay back against the bed with her.

"I love you, sissy. I know you're probably tired of me saying this, but I can't thank you enough."

"I know, sweetie. And, like I've been telling you, I'm happy to do it and I'm glad I'm able to. If I'd been one year older, I don't think they would've allowed it. But, as Mama used to say, 'What God has ordained can't be stopped'," said Bridgette.

"Amen, sis. I really wish Ivy could've been here to experience this with us. Maybe we should take a selfie and send it to her," said Savannah, reaching for her purse sitting on a nearby table and retrieving her iPhone. She saw the sour look on Bridgette's face when she positioned the phone's camera in front of them.

"Oh stop it, Bridgette. Both of you need to. I'm tired of this. This is such an exciting moment for us all, and we should be able to celebrate it together. So, come on and drop the sourpuss face," said Savannah, sticking out her tongue and making Bridgette laugh as she snapped the pic of them.

"See how easy that was?" she asked and then placed a kiss on her big sister's cheek.

Bridgette smiled and Savannah took more selfies of them. It was a heartwarming sister moment that neither of them would ever forget.

Chapter Twenty

"**Y**ou don't look too well. Actually, you're looking kind of green. Here drink this."

Bridgette took the bottle of water from her best friend and business partner, Fatima as they both stood in the small space of the bathroom in her office. Bridgette had just finished splashing her face with cold water and was drying it with a paper towel after vomiting in the toilet.

"Thanks, girl," Bridgette said as she tossed the used paper towel in a nearby trashcan and took the bottle from her. She twisted the cap off and took a long gulp.

"Do you want me to go and get you a ginger ale?" Fatima asked, rubbing her back. Bridgette shook her head. "No. I'll be fine. I'll make a cup of tea. That usually calms my stomach some," she said.

"You know you don't have to be here. You really should go on home and relax for the rest of the day. I'm here now, so you can give up control," Fatima offered and they both laughed as they walked back into the office to sit down.

Fatima and Bridgette had been best friends since seventh grade and throughout high school, even though they went to different colleges; Bridgette had stayed in state to go to

NC State University and Fatima had gone out-of-state to Texas Southern University, but distance hadn't broken their bond. And even though Fatima still lived miles away now in Miami, Florida with her husband and teenage daughter, they were still close. Fatima was like a third sister and she really was like a part of the family.

Bridgette had always talked about opening a bakery and when her boys had reached school age, she'd done just that with Fatima's encouragement since she herself owned several businesses. She'd guided Bridgette on everything she needed to know and even put up some of her own money to help her get started, making her more of a silent partner since she wouldn't be there on a daily basis to help run Sugar Rush. But a few times out of the year, she came to check on things, even though now, she was there for personal reasons than business. She was there to check on her best friend who was now three months pregnant with her sister's baby.

"I'm really glad you are and not because you're here at the bakery with me now, but for being here to support me," said Bridgette, smiling at her as they sat on the sofa in the corner of her office.

"I guess Nick was right," Bridgette said, chuckling.

"About what?" Fatima queried.

"That I must've been suffering from temporary insanity offering to carry my sister's baby. He said that to me when I told him I was going to do it," Bridgette said, taking another gulp of water.

Fatima shook her head with a disapproving look on her face. "Hopefully, he'll come back to his senses. I understand he has mixed feelings about it, but I really despise how he's been treating you. In all of the years you've been married to him, I've never known him to behave this way," said Fatima.

"Well, it doesn't help that his family has been in his ear about it, especially his mother. You know she's never been a big fan of mine. Now, he's completely convinced that I disregarded his feelings without any thought, and that's not what happened at all. I really did consider his concerns, but ultimately, it boiled down to how I would feel if I were in my sister's shoes. So, the decision was quite easy for me and I wish he could understand that," Bridgette said, her voice laced with sadness.

It hurt Bridgette that Nick seemed to be pulling away from her when she needed him the most. He wasn't talking to her much lately and it hadn't been from her lack of trying. She could truly say that this was the first time she really felt alone in their marriage, and she really didn't know what to do about it. She'd thought about suggesting they talk to the psychologist they'd been evaluated by for their pre-screening because she'd been easy to talk to and understanding to Nick's reservations, but decided against it. She had already asked enough of him with everything he'd had to go through as her spouse for her to get approved to be Savannah's surrogate, so she figured she'd give him time to come around on his own.

"And like I said, he has a right to feel like he wants to, but what's done is done. It's not like you can reverse it. He needs to man up and deal with it because last I checked you're still his wife who's pregnant, regardless of how it came to be.

And for that reason alone, he should support you and not be causing you any more stress than you've already placed on yourself in wanting to deliver your sister a healthy baby. I think it's such a selfless act and it really shows how much you love your family. If I had a sister, I don't think I could do it to be honest," said Fatima.

"Well, I really appreciate you saying that. I know it's unconventional," said Bridgette, making air quotes with her fingers, "but I wish everyone would look at the big picture. I'm bringing a life into this world for someone who can't. It's hard for me to see the problem with that when I know how much of a blessing it is."

"It is a blessing. Mama Ree and Mr. Eldridge would be so proud of you for what you're doing for Savannah. I know they're smiling down on you from heaven right now."

Her best friend's words brought tears to Bridgette's eyes for two reasons; she missed her parents dearly, especially her mother because they were so close, partly because she was Aretha Alston's first born and she'd doted on Bridgette from birth until she'd turned eight years old and Ivy came along.

Bridgette remembered how excited she'd been at having a baby sister. Even though she liked being an only child, it got lonely sometimes in the big old house they'd grown up in. She'd eagerly embraced sisterhood when Ivy came home and her new responsibilities as a big sister. She helped her mother make bottles, give Ivy baths and held her while she sat with their mother in Ivy's nursery as she sang her favorite hymn that always put Ivy to sleep.

It broke her heart that there was so much tension and discord between her and Ivy, and sadly, it had only worsened over the past few months. She'd been around more for Savannah throughout her recovery and treatment, and Bridgette was glad about that, but she wished that she could be there for her too, especially with her now being pregnant and the problems she was going through with Nick. She missed being able to call her up and talk and it seemed like those days were far from happening anytime soon. They could barely stand to be in one another's presence and if they had to be for too long, a silly argument always ensued. She was fighting with two of the people she loved the most and it was stressing her out, which wasn't good for her condition.

"I really hope so, Fatima. I've always tried to do right by my sisters because I'm the oldest. I know I can be overbearing sometimes and overprotective, but it's because I love them so much. They're like my babies and I'd do anything for those two girls," said Bridgette, swallowing back her tears.

Fatima rubbed her arm. "There's no doubt about that. The proof is in the proverbial oven," said Fatima, rubbing Bridgette's belly causing her to chuckle.

"I just wish that me and Ivy could find some common ground."

"I'm sure it will all work out. Families have disagreements sometimes, but what's important is that you work to move past them. And, I know you've been upset with Ivy, but you have to admit that she's always here when it matters most like now. She's been by Savannah's side just as much as you have. She loves you both. You all have to find a way to come together, especially now with this baby coming," said Fatima.

"I agree," Bridgette said, followed by a deep sigh. "I just don't know what to do about Nick, but I do know one thing, Fatima. I can't keep living like we're living. Things have to change."

"And I agree with you on that one," said Fatima

"I would've never thought that we'd be in such a bad place in our marriage. He barely utters more than a few words to me, and he acts as if the thought of me carrying this baby disgusts him. I mean he acts as if I got pregnant by another man or something," said Bridgette, taking another sip of water.

"Well, I don't know what else you can do that you already haven't," said Fatima.

"I've tried talking to him until I'm blue in the face, but it always leads to more arguing and I just don't want to deal with that anymore. I can't." Bridgette felt herself getting emotional again.

"And you shouldn't have to. It's not like you did this to hurt him in any way. You're just trying to help your sister, so I don't understand how he made this about him," said Fatima, rolling her eyes.

Bridgette could tell Fatima was getting riled up. She was one of those ride or die friends who always had her back.

"I'm just praying that we can survive this. I'm scared to say this because I don't want to put it out in the universe, but I hope he doesn't have an affair on me. We haven't been intimate because he acts like touching me would be committing a crime or something," said Bridgette, looking at her friend with sadness in her eyes.

"And he'd be a complete fool. You're the best thing that ever happened to Nicholas Harper and he needs to start acting as such. And if he does decide to go mess around with some thot, we both know a good divorce attorney," said Fatima, referring to her mother.

"Thot? Girl, you've been watching too many of those reality TV shows," Bridgette said and Fatima laughed. "I hope that I don't even have to entertain the thought of a divorce. I think Nick's ego is a bit bruised right now, but we're nowhere near that. We haven't had the perfect marriage, but we've always been able to work out our differences and I'm praying that he'll come around, especially before the boys start to notice the tension between us."

"I know what you mean. They're very impressionable at that age and perceptive. They pick up so much even when we don't think they do," said Fatima.

"Absolutely. That's why I haven't told them about the baby yet. I want them to be able to grasp fully what I'm doing and why. I think they'll understand, but I just want to wait for the right time. And, I know this is wishful thinking, but I want both Nick and I to talk with them about this. I don't want to have to do it alone."

"And you shouldn't have to. I'm really hoping that Nick will change his attitude soon because I'd hate to have to catch a case because of how he's been treating my best friend," said Fatima and then they both laughed.

"I know it's only for a few days, but again, I'm so glad you're here, Fatima. It's good to have someone I can talk to outside of the situation."

Fatima smiled at her. "You know I've always got your back. You're my A-one from day one."

"You sure got that right," said Bridgette. "I love you, girl."

"Love you, too. And, I know it's easier said than done, but try not to worry. Everything will work itself out. You're going to have a beautiful, healthy baby for your sister and even though Nick is not my favorite person right now, your marriage will be even stronger because of everything you're going through. I really believe that."

Bridgette pondered her best friend's words and prayed that what she was saying would be true.

Chapter Twenty-One

Savannah had been hospitalized twice from the side effects of chemotherapy and radiation that she'd been receiving simultaneously for the past ten weeks. It had been a harrowing couple of months with her battling severe fatigue and diarrhea and constant vomiting. Some days, she questioned how much more she could take because it was so bad, but she managed and she had her husband and sisters to thank. They'd really been taking care of her even though at first, she hadn't been the best patient. She'd been resistant to their constant presence, even lashing out at them a few times, but she realized they were just trying to be supportive. She knew it had to be just as hard on them as it was on her, especially Julius.

Their sex life or lack thereof had become almost torturous for Savannah because of the vaginal dryness and pain she experienced during their lovemaking. They'd had to get creative until her treatment was over and the symptoms subsided. Julius had been the epitome of sticking it out through "better or worse," which is why she couldn't wait for their baby to be born because that would surely bring them some happiness after all of the pain. In six more months, she'd be a mother, and every time she thought about that she felt an overwhelming sense of joy.

"What are you over there smiling about, Bubbling Brown Sugar?" Ivy asked, peering at her. She was driving Savannah to her radiation appointment. Thankfully, it was her last week of brachytheraphy, an internal form of radiation she'd been receiving twice a week for an additional three weeks after completing the external treatments. She'd be officially done with cervical cancer treatment at the end of the week.

"What? I didn't realize I was," Savannah responded.

"Like a Chess cat."

Savannah chuckled. "I was thinking about the baby coming. I love the way the nursery is turning out. I just need a white rocking chair like the one Mama had for us, so I can sit and sing him or her to sleep just the way she did."

"Her voice was so beautiful. I always told her she could've given Whitney, Mariah or Toni Braxton a run for their money. She was the true voice in the Alston household," said Ivy.

"Yes, sissy. The world had Aretha Franklin, but we had Aretha Alston," said Savannah and they both laughed.

"I miss that woman so much," said Savannah, her voice now somber.

"I do too. But, her spirit definitely surrounds us. I think that's why Bridgette and I haven't killed each other yet."

Savannah shook her head.

"I agree because nothing I say or do seems to be working and honestly, I don't have the energy to keep playing referee between you two."

"And nobody asked you to. I've told you time and time again to stay out of it. You have enough to deal with," said Ivy.

"Well, now Bridgette does also. So, please for my sake, resolve whatever issue you're having with her. I don't need her stressing about it, especially since she's carrying my baby."

"I'm not the one with the funky attitude, so she's the one with the issue. Not me," Ivy retorted with irritation. "I'm not going to kiss Bridgette's butt. Pregnant or not."

"That's not what I'm saying, Ivy so don't be so huffy and on the defensive. We should all be supporting one another now. I don't like the distance this is creating between us." Her sisters' issues were really weighing heavily on Savannah. She just didn't get why they couldn't get along. Savannah thought that everything they'd been through as a family would've drawn them closer, but it hadn't. It seemed to be getting worse.

They'd both been going to her treatment appointments, but Bridgette always met them there because as she told Savannah, she had no desire to be crammed in the tight space of a car with Ivy since they would surely get into an argument. Savannah knew it wasn't just the hormones of her sister being pregnant that was talking because that's all they'd been doing lately. It started when she began chemotherapy.

She could only have one person with her while she was getting her infusion and that first day, they'd got into a spat about which one of them it would be. Savannah was embarrassed at how they'd behaved, and even more so when Ivy had stormed out of the medical facility and called Bridgette out of her name, which thankfully she didn't hear. Savannah had to have them alternate days to cut back on all of the drama. Radiation was a little less stressful because even though they'd been told that Bridgette wouldn't be at any risk by being pregnant having contact with her, they'd both decided not to take any chances, so that just left Ivy.

Julius had attended most of the appointments as well, but the last few weeks, he'd been busy with another high profile case that kept him tied up in court most mornings when her appointments were scheduled, but he always called to check in on her when he could.

"Don't get upset. It's not that serious," said Ivy.

"But, it is, Ivy. We're all we have and if something happens to one of us, the other two would have to be there for the other," said Savannah with sadness. She felt her tears coming, but fought to hold them back. Her sisters' behavior was frustrating, and in her opinion, they were both acting like kids.

"Don't talk like that, Savannah. Nothing's going to happen to anybody. We're all going to be around for a long time getting on each other's nerves even as old ladies like *The Golden Girls*. And I'm going to get a kick out of seeing Bridgette get there first since she's so much older," said Ivy and that made Savannah chuckle. *The Golden Girls* was one of their favorite TV shows.

"You're so wrong for that. But, seriously, this battle I've had with cancer has really made me appreciate everything about my life. It's nothing I would've imagined I'd be going through, and it made me realize just how short life is and all of the things we take for granted. We never think about those things until we're at risk of losing them. We have to do better, Ivy. As a family and as a sisterhood."

Ivy reached over and clasped her hand over Savannah's to comfort her.

"I agree. And even though I don't think I've done anything to warrant Bridgette's ornery attitude toward me, I'll be the bigger person and extend the olive branch. So, are you happy now, spoiled behind?" Ivy joked and a smile spread across Savannah's face.

"I love you, Bubbling-Brown-Su-gah," she sang, making Savannah laugh.

"You're a mess, but I love you just the same," said Savannah, adjusting the silk scarf tied around her head that she'd been wearing since her hair began to fall out, shortly after starting chemo. She hadn't become completely bald, but it had come out in patches and she didn't want to wear a wig, so Ivy had brought her back a bunch of designer scarves she'd gotten specially made for Savannah by some famous, fashion designer she used to work for in New York. Ivy would wear them too in support of her like she was now.

"We have to take a selfie so I can post it on Instagram," Ivy said, when they got to Carolinas Medical Center where Savannah received her radiation. They posed cheek-to-cheek pursing their lips into those ridiculous duck lips when Ivy snapped the photo. She had over a million followers on Instagram, and they'd become invested in Savannah's recovery, posting words of encouragement and support. It was touching, and it was one more thing that gave Savannah comfort. Now, if only her sisters would show that same kind of love to one another. She would keep her fingers crossed that Ivy kept her word and made things right within their sisterhood.

Chapter Twenty-Two

Later in the week, Bridgette walked in her house and heard a voice coming from the kitchen and frowned. *I know good and doggone well…*she thought as she approached closer with her twin boys in tow after picking them up from school. Dylan, the oldest by two minutes raced toward the source of the familiar voice, humming what sounded like an old Shirley Caesar song, the same as her mother used to.

"Grandma," he shouted, running over to the gray-haired, sixty-something-year old woman, sitting at the kitchen island with one hand wrapped around a Heineken beer bottle and the other gripping a pen with a crossword puzzle book in front of her.

"There go my little boogers. Come give granny a big ole hug," said Bridgette's mother-in-law, Cassietta, rising from the bar stool she was sitting on and wrapping her arms around both boys. She eyed Bridgette with a disapproving look. "Bridgette," she said in a flat attempt at a greeting.

"Cassietta, what are you doing here?" Bridgette matched her tone. She had no desire to deal with her mother-in-law today, especially with the way she was feeling. Being pregnant at forty was definitely different than when she was in her thirties. She'd planned to get dinner started and then get the boys started on their homework while she finished, but from the savory smell of tomato sauce wafting throughout the kitchen and the two large pots on the stove, it was obvious Cassietta had that taken care of.

"Do I need permission to come and check on my family?" Cassietta queried, a hand on her hip, but Bridgette didn't reply. She knew Cassietta was there to insinuate herself into her and Nick's business. She was the quintessential, meddling mother-in-law.

"Grandma, did you make spaghetti and meatballs?" Ryan, the youngest twin asked with excitement.

"I sure did. You know I have to make my babies their favorite foods while I'm here. I've got a batch of my chocolate fudge brownies baking in the oven right now for dessert," said Cassietta with a big grin on her face.

"Yaayyyy!!! Brownies," both boys yelped in anticipation as if their mother didn't bring them enough baked goods from her bakery.

Cassietta's hearty laughter rang throughout the large space of the kitchen. "I love it," she said with just as much excitement.

"Boys, go ahead upstairs and get started on your homework. I'll be up in a minute," Bridgette instructed.

The boys gave their grandmother one last hug before grabbing their book bags they'd tossed by the entrance and raced upstairs one behind the other. Bridgette sat her purse on the island, surveying the kitchen before addressing her mother-in-law who'd taken her place back at the island grabbing her beer and taking a swig.

"How long have you been here?" Bridgette asked.

"Well, long enough to start up a few loads of that laundry you've got backed up from here to yonder and cook dinner," Cassietta remarked and Bridgette didn't like the implication she heard, but decided to ignore it. She didn't have the energy to go back and forth with her.

"I appreciate it, but I wish you would've let me know that you were coming," said Bridgette, walking over to the refrigerator, pulling out a bottle of water and twisting the cap off.

"My son knew I was coming. Why didn't you?" she asked. Now, sitting with her arms folded and staring at her.

Bridgette sighed and took a drink of water. She knew Cassietta was aware of their marital problems, so why she was trying to be facetious Bridgette didn't know, but she wasn't in the mood for it, especially since she was part of the problem.

"Well, your son doesn't have a lot to say to me these days, so how would I know," Bridgette retorted, making her way back to the island and sitting down at the other end, away from her mother-in-law. "But, of course you know that already," she added.

"Despite what you think, Bridgette, he hasn't told me much of anything because I suspect that he doesn't want me to insert my two cents about this whole situation you've created."

Bridgette shook her head. "Oh, you don't have to because you've already done that. Let you tell it, I'm trying to play God," Bridgette retorted, her voice dripping with sarcasm and shaking her head because she was still in disbelief at some of the things Cassietta had said to her when she learned what Bridgette was planning to do for her sister. She took another sip of her water, ignoring her mother-in-law's glare.

"And I'll say it again. It's just plain, ole wrong to insert yourself into God's will. And, not only that, but how do you expect a man to feel watching his wife walk around with another man's baby growing in her stomach? I don't care if your sister's DNA is part of it. That makes it even more sickening, if you ask me," she said, her voice filled with disgust and going up an octave.

It was Bridgette's turn to glare at her mother-in-law.

"Will you keep your voice down, Cassietta? I don't want the boys to hear you," Bridgette hissed.

Cassietta sat back in her seat and shook her head. "Ummph...ummph...ummph. These are truly some praying times. You haven't even clued them in on this foolishness yet? And that's another reason why it's a bad idea. Have you even thought about how those babies are going to feel about this? What happens when you come home from the hospital without a baby that they'll obviously see you carrying here soon? No matter how you try and explain it, it'll still be hard for them to understand."

"Why don't you let me worry about that, Cassietta," Bridgette huffed.

Cassietta threw her hands up. "Fine. I've said my peace about it—," Cassietta remarked before Bridgette cut her off from finishing her statement.

"I certainly hope for the last time. I'm clear on how you feel about it along with your son," Bridgette said. "Now, how long are you planning on being here?"

"Probably for a few days, but it may be longer. I haven't decided yet. It's obvious you need some help around here with yet another thing you've added on," Cassietta said, her eyes resting temporarily on Bridgette's belly, a small mound beginning to form there. Bridgette sighed and prayed silently for the strength to deal with her mother-in-law and her husband who now had a live-in ally for the next few days or however long she decided to be there. Bridgette hoped she would leave sooner rather than later for all of their sakes.

Chapter Twenty-Three

Bridgette had just left her boys' bedroom, checking to see if they were actually in their beds and not on their iPads as they sometimes were, but they were sound asleep. She'd kissed them and tucked them under the covers extra tight, even though she knew that by morning both sets of bedding would be on the floor. Now, she was in her pajamas and sipping chamomile tea while reading *Jezebel's Daughter*, the latest novel by one of her favorite authors, Jacquelin Thomas. It was a welcomed reprieve from her mother-in-law and husband, especially after the evening she'd had with them.

She'd felt like an outsider in her own home and it wasn't a pleasant feeling. They'd basically ignored her at dinner, talking and laughing with one another along with the boys as if she wasn't sitting at the table. It was hard for Bridgette to refrain from rolling her eyes the entire time or even dismissing herself altogether, but she wouldn't give them the satisfaction. However, it was time for her to talk with Nick about his behavior, and she didn't care if he wanted to or not. He wasn't going to keep telling her that he didn't feel like talking about it. Things had to change between them because she wouldn't tolerate it any longer. Either he acted like he wanted to be her husband or he could make other living arrangements.

Bridgette hated the thought of a separation, but the tension between them was causing her an added amount of stress that she didn't need to deal with. It was as if they were roommates instead of the married couple that they were, and if they were going to make it another ten years, there needed to be some serious attitude adjustments. Well, at least on Nick's part anyway. She still tried to be the loving wife she'd always been, but his ego was getting in the way of that and creating distance between them.

After reading a few chapters of her book, Bridgette removed her red-framed eyeglasses and placed them on the nightstand. She'd been anticipating Nick coming to bed so she could talk to him, but it was apparent that he was still sitting up with his mother in an attempt to avoid her. She also knew that she was probably the topic of their conversation. She'd left them downstairs a few hours ago after putting away the leftovers from dinner and cleaning up the kitchen, which neither of them offered to help, but instead they'd gone out on the deck with Heinekens and Bridgette guessed they were still out there. She had a mind to march down there and demand he come to bed, but she didn't want to appear desperate for his attention.

Bridgette grabbed the remote lying next to her on the bed and flipped to the Food Network, hoping he'd be up soon. After about twenty minutes into the TV show she was watching, Nick came strolling in the bedroom and Bridgette didn't waste any time. She'd been waiting long enough and now she was sitting with her arms folded across her chest, glaring at him.

"Nick, we need to talk," she announced and she saw the deep rise and fall of his chest from sighing followed by a shake of his head.

"I'm tired, Bridgette and I just want to hop in the shower and then get to sleep," he replied, sitting on the edge of his side of the bed with his back to her and removing his shoes.

"Well, this won't take long. I don't appreciate how you've been treating me lately and I certainly don't appreciate you not giving me the consideration of letting me know that your mother was coming for a visit."

"It slipped my mind." He stood to remove his jeans.

"Nicholas Harper, I won't play these games with you. You need to stop acting like a child and act like the forty-year-old man that you are. I'm tired of it. I'm already raising two children and you're acting like a third," Bridgette said.

"Well, the difference between me and them is that you can't control how I act. I'm a grown man, Bridgette."

"Well, then act like it," Bridgette yelled, not meaning to, but she didn't care because she'd had enough of his attitude. "What kind of a man walks around the house giving his wife the silent treatment?" she added.

Nick inhaled deeply and then exhaled like he was trying to keep his composure. "You need to calm down and watch how you speak to me. Who's acting like a child now throwing a temper tantrum because things aren't going how you want them to? Did you really expect me not to feel some type of way about this whole situation? You didn't care about my feelings then, so why should I care now about yours?" Nick said, matter-of-factly, removing his Hampton t-shirt, the school he'd attended for his Master's degree.

"I did care about your feelings, Nick, and I do now. We've talked about this. And if I remember correctly, you said that you understood. You went through the screening and signed the surrogacy agreement, now, you've done a complete one-eighty and I don't understand it. Well, I have an idea and she's a floor below us," said Bridgette, referring to her mother-in-law.

Nick guffawed like he'd done when she first told him she wanted to be her sister's surrogate, and it annoyed her then like it did now. She hated it because it sounded as if he was making fun of her like what she was saying was so ridiculous.

"Leave my mother out of this. She has nothing to do with it," he said, shaking his head.

"Why have you been giving me the cold shoulder then? You're really making this whole thing difficult and it doesn't have to be. It's only temporary."

"You say that like I'm supposed to just deal with it and that should be the end of it. You can always do what you want because I'll always go with the flow, but I'm tired of you trying to play me, Bridgette. I'm nobody's fool," he said, glaring at her. "So, if you're expecting any more support than I've already given. Don't. Because I'm done with it all," he said with finality as he walked to the master bathroom and slammed the door behind him.

Bridgette burst into tears, overwhelmed with frustration.

Chapter Twenty-Four

The next morning, after her argument with Nick and once again, not getting much sleep and waking up with a gnawing headache, Bridgette got up to make breakfast, but found Cassietta in the kitchen already cooking, and her presence angered Bridgette.

"You don't have to cook every meal in this house, Cassietta," Bridgette snapped at her mother-in-law, reaching around her and snatching the teakettle off the stove to fill it with water for tea. She was feeling more nauseous than normal.

"Hmmph, I guess the symptoms of pregnancy are in full effect this morning with your crankiness, but they're directed at the wrong person. I certainly didn't get you pregnant, but neither did my son," Cassietta said and Bridgette wanted to smack that annoying smirk off of her face.

"You know what, Cassietta? I've had just about enough of your snide and rude comments. You don't get to disrespect me in my own house, especially since I pay the mortgage," Bridgette said, filling the teakettle with water. She didn't want to have to go there, but she was tired of both her mother-in-law and her husband's disrespectful behavior toward her.

"And you mention that to prove what, Bridgette? That you're in control? That might work with my son, but I couldn't care less about it. So what you bought this big ole house just to prove that you could. You've spent your entire marriage doing that and I don't know how much longer you think Nicholas is going to allow you to keep it up. My guess is not too much longer, considering this last foolish act you've done," Cassietta remarked, flipping French toast on a griddle.

"Oh, you'd just love that wouldn't you?" Bridgette slammed the teakettle back onto the stove before turning on the burner. "I'm too much of a woman for your liking. I'm not like your other daughter-in-law. I'm not Suzy Homemaker. I actually have a brain and goals and a life of my own."

She liked her sister-in-law, Yvette and she wasn't trying to degrade her in any way, but they were two different women, especially with how they approached their marriages. Yvette was a stay-at-home mother to three young daughters that she'd had late in life because Nick's older brother, Vincent had wanted to wait—for whatever reason he'd given her. Bridgette had never bothered to ask her, but she suspected it was because he was trying to keep up with all of those women he slept around on her with, but Bridgette would never tell her that. And now, in her late-forties, her daily life consisted of changing diapers, making bottles, cooking three meals a day and opening her legs wide anytime her husband wanted her to.

Bridgette found it to be a travesty because Yvette was a smart woman who'd graduated with high honors from Duke

University and had plans of becoming a doctor, until she met Vincent. Then, her dreams of stethoscopes and curing sick patients disappeared like the slim waistline she once had. All she did now, was chase babies around the house and with what little downtime she had, she spent it in front of the TV snacking. It was really sad, but that was her life and certainly not Bridgette's and never would be.

"Oh. I see. So, you think you're better than Yvette? She actually puts her family first like a real woman is supposed to, and that makes her more of a woman than you'll ever be," Cassietta spat, stacking French toast on a plate next to her on the counter.

Bridgette was so mad that she felt like steam was about to blow out of her ears. She was about to tell her mother-in-law what she could do with her opinions when Nick rushed into the kitchen.

"What's going on in here? I could hear you two as I was coming down the stairs," he demanded, his brows furrowed. "And, if I can hear you, the boys certainly will be able to."

Bridgette looked at him with disgust. After the way Nick had spoken to her last night and pretty much told her that she was alone in their marriage, he was the last person she wanted to see right now. She could barely sleep next to him after their argument, but she'd been too exhausted and heartbroken to get out of bed and walk down the hall to the guest bedroom. But tonight, he would be the one sleeping in there or in a hotel—she didn't care which.

"It's time for your mother to go back to Durham. I can't deal with the both of you anymore. It's making me sick," Bridgette huffed.

Cassietta shook her head and began cracking eggs into a large ceramic bowl.

"I'll leave when I get ready to and nobody's going to tell me otherwise," Cassietta said, strolling to the refrigerator like she dared anyone to say anything to her and removing a bottle of milk.

Bridgette placed a hand on her hip and glowered at Nick, ignoring her mother-in-law's remark.

"Either she leaves or the both of you can. I won't stand for the judgment and disrespect anymore. From either of you. I'm done," Bridgette announced, now teary-eyed.

"Stop being dramatic, Bridgette. I'm not going anywhere and neither is my mother, so just stop while you're ahead," Nick countered, his eyes challenging her, but Bridgette wasn't going to back down.

"Try me.. Just try me," Bridgette shouted, tears now rolling down her face.

"You need to calm down. I've warned you about how you speak to me. I don't yell at you, so don't do it to me."

Cassietta shook her head and said something under her breath that Bridgette couldn't hear, but she knew whatever it was, it was probably directed at her. She'd always tried to respect her elders because that was how she was raised, but Cassietta was going to be the exception if she kept pushing her.

"You deal with your mother then or I will. And neither of you will like it," Bridgette threatened and that caused Cassietta to turn around and glare at her. She planted both hands on her hips like she was ready for battle, and Bridgette was going to oblige her.

"And what is that supposed to mean? I know you don't have the gall to be threatening me because baby, I can promise you, this ain't what you want," said Cassietta. "Don't let my age fool you or the fact that I'm saved. I can still deliver a Bull City beat down."

"I'd like to see you try it," Bridgette said, moving toward her and Nick stepped between them.

"You really don't think I'm going to let you run up on my mother? Are you serious right now, Bridgette? You need to calm yourself down. Now," Nick bellowed.

Bridgette did something that she'd never thought she would ever do to her husband, she raised her open palm and slapped him as hard as she could, causing him to grab her wrist and squeeze it, hurting her.

"You let go of me. Right. Now," Bridgette shouted, crying uncontrollably now.

"Not until you calm down. I mean it, Bridgette," he said.

"Let her go, Nicholas. Let that heifer run up on me. She won't run up on anybody else. And I don't care about her being pregnant. She got me bent," Cassietta barked from behind Nick's back.

Bridgette was about to swing another blow at Nick with her free hand when she felt pain in her abdomen, causing her to yelp. She snatched her wrist out of Nick's grasp and placed her hands on her stomach. She kneeled over from the pain and discomfort she felt.

"Bridgette, what's wrong?" Nick asked, his anger now replaced with deep concern. He bent down to her level, his hand rested on the small of her back.

"I think it's the baby. Oh. God. I can't lose this baby," Bridgette cried and then, she saw the blood dripping down her leg as she heard the whistle of the teakettle.

Chapter Twenty-Five

Savannah and Ivy were having breakfast courtesy of Julius before he'd left, headed to court. Today, she would be receiving her final radiation treatment and as she had been, Ivy was going to take her to her appointment that afternoon since he'd be in court all day. She couldn't wait to get it over with, and hopefully, it would be the last time she had to endure it. She knew the road to recovery was just beginning, but at least this part would be behind her.

"It's a shame Julius doesn't have a twin brother because if I had a man like him I might reconsider my stance on marriage," Ivy joked, enjoying the Western omelet her brother-in-law had made.

Savannah chuckled. "That man is one of a kind. Fashioned by God just for me," said Savannah, biting into a piece of wheat toast.

" Halle-lu-jer," said Ivy, raising a palm in the air and mimicking the infamous Tyler Perry grandmother, Madea.

Savannah laughed. "You're a fool." She loved having her sister around. She really kept her spirits up, especially since she'd woken up feeling a bit down.

She was missing being at school and around her students. School had resumed a month prior in August and Savannah hated that she wasn't there to welcome her students back, but she was hoping to return in a few months when she was better. She knew some people going through similar treatment could go right back to work, but the extreme side effects wouldn't allow her to just yet.

Everyone at the elementary school had been so supportive and many of her students had sent her homemade cards they'd drawn for her to get well. It really warmed Savannah's heart to know they'd been thinking about her. She really missed seeing their little faces every day and she couldn't wait to see them again and get back to her daily work routine.

They were finishing breakfast when Savannah's landline rang. "I wonder who that could be. It's fairly early," she mused.

"I don't know. It could be your sister. She's prone to making early morning calls," said Ivy, taking a sip from her coffee mug.

That thought made Savannah hurry to answer the phone. "Hello?" she answered.

"Uhh…Savannah?" the deep voice on the other end responded.

"Nick?" Savannah queried, her face now set in a deep frown. She didn't like the tone in his voice or the fact that he was even calling her; especially with the way he'd been treating her sister. But, even though he certainly hadn't been her favorite person lately, she couldn't help to feel a little responsible for why there was strife in their marriage, but if his behavior had caused something to happen to Bridgette or her baby—*Oh God, the baby*, she thought, as she began to panic. The look on her face caused Ivy to stand and rush to her.

"Savannah? What is it? Who is that?" Ivy asked.

"What is it, Nick? Is Bridgette okay?" Savannah asked, her voice barely a whisper now.

"*Bridgette?* What's going on, Savannah? What is he saying?" Ivy badgered. She now had her ear pressed against the phone trying to listen in on what was being said.

"She—well, uh—she," Nick stammered.

"For Christ's sake, Nick. Tell me what's going on. Is my sister okay?" Savannah yelled at him, her patience gone.

Ivy placed a hand on her chest at Savannah's reaction.

"We're at the hospital. She was having real bad pain in her abdomen—"

Savannah dropped the phone before he could finish his statement.

"We've got to get to the hospital," she said, tears filling her eyes.

"Savannah, what happened?" Ivy demanded. And then she picked up the phone from the floor. "Hello. Nick? Are you still there?" she shouted into the phone. Her eyes rested on Savannah who was now shaking. "What's going on? Where are you?"

Savannah saw the color in her sister's face change and she knew Bridgette had miscarried her baby.

Chapter Twenty-Six

Bridgette laid in the hospital bed feeling like the worst person in the world. She felt like a failure. She'd lost her sister's baby and she didn't know how to accept that fact. It was her fault that Savannah's dreams of motherhood had once again been shattered, and this time she'd have someone to blame.

Bridgette's eyes were red and puffy because she'd been crying since the doctor told her that she'd miscarried the baby, and when she'd asked him why, he'd said that it could have been a multitude of reasons, but nothing he could pinpoint single handedly. This was the worst news that Bridgette could hear because to her, it felt like it was something she'd done, and she knew it boiled down to all the stress she'd been dealing with at home. And then, that witch Nick called a mother. If it hadn't been for them, she'd still be pregnant. No one would ever convince her of anything different, which is why she refused to have Nick anywhere near her.

He'd rushed her to the hospital when she'd collapsed in the kitchen and when she'd seen the blood dripping from her leg; Bridgette knew that she was in danger of losing the baby. Cassietta had acted like she was concerned; trying to come to her aide, but Bridgette had recoiled. She didn't want that woman anywhere near her ever again if she could help it. The only thing she was grateful to her for was that she'd made sure the boys hadn't come downstairs to witness any of what was happening. Bridgette didn't want to traumatize them in any way.

She had been praying since she'd received the unfortunate news about the miscarriage, that Savannah would be able to forgive her for losing the baby. She'd even planned to go through the entire process all over again, even though it was grueling and expensive if that was what her sister wanted. She thought back to when she'd told Savannah she was pregnant, and fresh tears sprang to her eyes as she remembered how happy she was because it had been right after one of her daily radiation treatments.

"You feeling okay?" Bridgette had asked her from the driver's seat of her SUV. They were in the parking garage of the hospital getting ready to leave.

"I'm feeling fine. At least for right now," Savannah said.

Bridgette reached over and squeezed her hand.

"Well, I have some news that I know you'll love to hear," said Bridgette with a wide smile.

"What's that?" Savannah asked.

"You're going to be a mother, little sissy," Bridgette announced, rubbing her stomach.

Tears filled Savannah's eyes immediately.

"Oh my God," Savannah exclaimed, her hand to her mouth in surprise. "Are you sure, Bridgette?"

"Absolutely, sweetie. I took two pregnancy tests to be sure. I know we have to confirm it in a few days when I go in for my appointment with Dr. Billingsley, but I know it will be positive."

"Wow. I can't believe this is actually going to happen. God has answered my prayers," Savannah mused, tears escaping her eyes.

"It's a wonderful blessing, honey. And I can't be more happier about it," said Bridgette, her own eyes filling with tears. Savannah reached over from the driver's seat to embrace her big sister.

"I love you so much, Bridgette. I'll never be able to thank you enough for making such a sacrifice for my husband and me. I'm eternally grateful," said Savannah.

"I love you too, sissy. And you don't have to thank me. I'd do it again and again if you wanted me to," Bridgette remarked.

And she'd meant every word. She wiped her tears as the nurse walked into the room to check her vitals.

Chapter Twenty-Seven

It sounded like a bad scene from a reality TV show. Bridgette heard yelling and some sort of a commotion right outside her hospital room.

"What in the world is going on?" Fatima asked, frowning. She was sitting in a chair next to Bridgette's bed.

Bridgette shrugged.

"I don't know, but it doesn't sound good. Sounds like a fight is going on out there," she replied.

Fatima stood.

"Let me go see what's going on. This is a hospital for crying out loud," she said, shaking her head.

"Girl, be careful," Bridgette warned her best friend. "Could be some crazy person on the loose."

Bridgette watched Fatima as she walked to the door and opened it to see if she could find out what was going on.

"Lord, have mercy," Fatima exclaimed.

"What is it?" Bridgette asked.

Fatima looked back at her with a horrified expression on her face.

"Girl, it's your sisters," Fatima said.

"What?" Bridgette exclaimed as she tried to rise up in bed, but then winced from the pain in her stomach.

"Be careful, Bridgette," Fatima fussed.

"What's going on?" Bridgette asked, as anxiety crept through her body. "Are they fighting?"

Fatima turned her attention back to the scene unfolding outside.

"Jesus, fix it," Fatima said.

"Fatima, will you tell me what's going on before I get out of this hospital bed and find out myself. What's going on with my sisters?"

"It looks like they've had some sort of altercation with Nick. I see two security guards standing between the three of them," Fatima said.

Bridgette rose gingerly from her laying position, wincing. Fatima looked back at her and rushed to her side to prevent her from hurting herself.

"Bridgette, what are you doing? You don't think I'm getting ready to let you get out of this bed," Fatima chastised her.

"But, I have to see what's going on with my family. I can't let them kill each other," Bridgette cried, now hysterical.

"No. You're going to stay right here. You're in no condition to be inserting yourself into any drama. I don't care who it is," Fatima chided.

"This is all my fault."

Fatima shushed her, rubbing her arm to try and calm her down.

"Nothing is your fault, love. They're all adults and responsible for their own behavior. They shouldn't be acting like that in public, especially a hospital that's full of sick people," Fatima said, shaking her head in disapproval.

"This is bad, Fatima. I've never seen this family so broken. And, I don't know how to fix it," Bridgette lamented through her tears.

"All I can say at this point, is give it to God," said Fatima.

Her best friend's words reminded Bridgette of a similar saying of her mother's.

"You just have to let go and let God, baby." Aretha Alston would say to her oldest daughter when she worried about things, especially of which she had no control.

Bridgette cried harder thinking about her mother. She missed her more than ever now. She needed to hear her say those comforting words. She needed her guidance. If she were here, she would've made it all better because Bridgette was failing at everything. She was failing in her marriage, failing in her sisterhood and failing to hold on to her sanity.

Chapter Twenty-Eight

When they'd reached the floor of the hospital Bridgette was on and stepped off the elevator and walked the short distance to get to her room, Ivy hadn't anticipated what would happen if they saw her brother-in-law. But, she never expected Savannah to attack him. It surprised Ivy because she'd never seen Savannah lift her hand to anyone. Ever. She just wasn't a violent person; she was an elementary school principal for Christ's sake, and usually had better control of her emotions. Normally, she was the peacemaker and mediator.

Ivy knew she was angry with Nick, and Savannah had talked about how she knew he was the reason Bridgette had lost her baby during their drive to Carolinas Medical Center, so when they rounded the corner and saw him sitting in the small waiting area not far from the hospital rooms, Savannah charged him before Ivy realized what was happening, hurling a few obscenities at him along the way. He'd been drinking coffee out of a Styrofoam cup, which slipped out of his hand, the hot liquid spilling down the front of his shirt and pants. He yelped out in pain, and Ivy didn't know if it was from the temperature of the coffee or the force of Savannah's hands as she made contact with his face and head.

There were a handful of people sitting in the waiting area, a few of them looked on in horror and the others scrambled to take refuge from the frail-looking, angry, black woman with the silk scarf tied around her head. And with everything she'd been through over the last few months physically, Ivy didn't know where she found so much strength.

"Savannah, stop it. Right now," Ivy chastised, pulling Savannah away from Nick who'd jumped to his feet, putting his forearms up in defense to block her blows.

"I know you're the reason my sister's in this hospital and why my baby's gone. I'll never forgive you, Nick," Savannah yelled at him.

Nick looked baffled and confused. He ran his hands down the front of his wet, stained shirt, shaking his head. "You need to calm down, Savannah," he said, through gritted teeth, glaring at his sister-in-law.

Savannah charged him again, but Ivy prevented her from making any more physical contact with him.

"Savannah, please," Ivy begged. "This isn't the time or the place."

Just then, two burly security guards came rushing up, a younger white man and an older black man.

"What's going on here?" the black security guard with a stomach that looked as big as two football fields, plunging over the top of his black uniform pants, inquired; Sizing them all up.

"There's just been a little misunderstanding," Nick said, his eyes glued on Savannah as if he wasn't sure if she'd go on the attack again.

The second of the two peered at Savannah, who was panting and had tears streaming down her face. Ivy held on to her sister, hoping she calmed down. She looked like she wanted to claw Nick's eyes out and Ivy had no doubt she would have if given the chance.

"Ma'am, are you all right?" he asked Savannah.

"She's fine," Ivy answered instead.

"We were called up here because of some sort of altercation. As you all know, this is a hospital and we can't have these types of disturbances. I'm going to have to ask y'all to leave," the second one said.

"I'm not going anywhere. Our sister is here and we're here to see her. If anybody is going to leave, that piece of sh—," Savannah yelled, trying to break free from Ivy's grip to charge at Nick again, causing the second guard to stand between the three of them.

"Ma'am, I'm going to need for you to calm down," the security guard warned.

"Savannah, stop this. You're going to get us thrown out of here. Is that what you want?" Ivy chided.

Savannah buried her face in her sister's chest and sobbed. Ivy hugged her tightly, she felt like a fragile child in her arms.

"I'm sorry, but again, I'm going to have to ask that you all leave. At least until everyone has calmed down and tempers aren't so high," the second security guard said.

Nick shook his head, and without another word or glance at his two sisters-in-law, he left the waiting area, turning the corner to head to the elevators.

"Savannah," Ivy spoke gently to her sister. "We'll go and do your radiation treatment, and if you're feeling up to it afterwards, we'll come back to see Bridgette."

Savannah didn't respond, but continued to sob. Ivy glared at the two security guards still standing there waiting for them to leave. She led her sister out of the waiting area, herself shaken up by everything that had happened. Both of her sisters were heartbroken, and it pained Ivy. She knew that they were going to need her, and for the first time in their sisterhood, she was going to have to be the anchor. A role she wasn't familiar with. She didn't know how she was going to do it, but she had no choice. As she held on to her sister, she prayed for strength not only for herself, but for all three of them.

Chapter Twenty-Nine

I vy's mind reeled as she sat in the waiting area in the cancer unit of the hospital while Savannah received her last radiation treatment. She still couldn't believe what had gone down. She knew it was early, but she needed a drink, and not her usual red wine—something strong and stiff. She had a bottle of Belvedere vodka chilling in her freezer at her condo and it was calling her name, but for right now she decided to head down to the cafeteria and grab something to eat. Not because she was hungry, but she just needed different scenery. Everybody sitting in the waiting area looked morbid—she included.

Ivy hated hospitals and what they represented for her. As a youngster, she was made to believe that they helped cure and fix people, that is until she'd lost both of her parents in this very hospital and thus, her confidence in the medical industry. And now, her sisters were here and it made her uneasy. She'd preferred to be anywhere else, like a beautiful beach in the Caribbean with one of those fruity, colorful cocktails, but she didn't have much of a choice. She was now going to have to be responsible for someone other than herself, and that made her want to drink even more.

After purchasing a turkey sandwich and bottle of water, Ivy found a table in the cafeteria amongst the lunchtime crowd that was starting to form and sat down. She thought about calling Bridgette to check on her, but decided to wait. It would be better to see her in person, especially since they hadn't been getting along lately. She could only imagine what she was going through. Ivy knew her big sister was blaming herself and feeling bad about losing Savannah's baby. She'd probably be carrying around a lot of guilt for a long time.

Ivy still wasn't sure if Bridgette had made the right decision in the first place to make such a sacrifice, but whatever her reasons were, Ivy couldn't help but to respect her even more. She'd always said she'd do anything for them, and she'd certainly proved it being her sister's surrogate and putting her own life, health and marriage at risk. But, that was who Bridgette was. Ivy thought back to one of the scariest times in her life, two years ago.

Ivy had been dating Lawrence for about nine months when she found out he was married and then she abruptly ended it. She'd moved on with her life, and hadn't thought much more about him, that is until his wife showed up at her front door three months later on a cold November evening, two days before Thanksgiving. Bridgette had been there because they were finalizing the details for their feast since it was Ivy's turn to host that year.

"Are you Ivy Alston?" the woman inquired, staring Ivy up and down.

Ivy frowned at the woman standing on her front porch. "Who wants to know?" she asked.

"I take that as a 'yes'," the woman said, shoving past Ivy into her foyer.

"What do you think you're doing? You can't just come in my house uninvited," Ivy said, surprised at the woman's boldness.

"I think I have every right to since you've been sleeping with my husband." She turned and snarled at Ivy, causing her to backup a few inches. The woman was standing so close in her face, Ivy could feel her breath.

"Who is your husband?" Ivy asked.

The woman snickered in disgust. "Don't play games with me. I'm not one to be toyed with, honey. And you'll see that soon enough." The woman glared at Ivy with cold, steely eyes that made her blood chill.

Instinct told Ivy that something wasn't right about this woman and here she was cornered between her and the front door in the small space of her foyer. She began forming an escape plan in her head.

"Who are you and what do you want? I don't want any trouble," Ivy said, keeping her eyes on the woman who looked like she was going to scratch Ivy's eyes out at any second.

"My name is Karma. And you know what they say about her. And today, you'll get yours," she said, pulling out a box cutter from the back pocket of her jeans.

Ivy screamed. Bridgette came running from the kitchen where they'd been prior to Ivy answering the door.

"Ivy, are you all right?" Bridgette shouted before seeing what was unfolding.

The woman turned in her direction, surprised that someone else was there.

"What the heck is going on? Who are y—," Bridgette's voice trailed off at the sight of the sharp blade of the box cutter.

Both she and Ivy seemed to be frozen in place. Ivy's heart was pounding so hard, she could hear the thumping in her ears. If the woman was bothered by Bridgette's unexpected presence she didn't show it. In fact, she seemed unfazed, as she stepped closer to Ivy.

"I'm going to teach you a lesson about opening your legs to married men. When I'm done with you, my husband nor any other man is going to want you for that matter," the woman snarled, aiming the blade at Ivy's vaginal area, causing her to let out a bloodcurdling scream.

But before the crazed woman could follow through with her plans to give Ivy a female circumcision, Bridgette came to her rescue. She eased up behind the woman and grabbed her arm, wrestling with her to get the box cutter out of her grip, but the woman was stronger and turned the deadly weapon on Bridgette, almost slicing her thumb off.

Ivy screamed in horror as she watched blood spew out of her sister's hand and drip down onto the hardwood floor, but Bridgette kept fighting even though she was badly injured. When the woman charged at Bridgette again, Ivy snapped out of her panicked state, realizing that her sister was in grave danger and could lose her life trying to save hers. She would never be able to forgive herself if something happened to her sister because of something she had nothing to do with.

Ivy grabbed the only thing she could use as a weapon at her disposal, her large sorority umbrella from the holder by the front door and began hitting the woman with it, not caring where her *blows landed, catching the woman off guard and causing her to lose her grip on her weapon. When it hit the floor, all three women lunged for it, but Bridgette got to it first. Now, defenseless and outnumbered, the woman made a hasty escape out the front door, pushing Ivy into a table on her way out, causing her to wince in pain from the impact to her back.*

Ivy had walked away with minor bruises, but Bridgette had to be taken to the hospital by ambulance for her severely injured hand where she received several stitches and would have a permanent scar. Luckily, she didn't have any nerve damage, which was a blessing.

After filing a report with police, Ivy found out who the woman was. Tessa Baxter was her name and she was indeed Lawrence's wife. She was apprehended a few days later and charged with assault with a deadly weapon. Even though Ivy had broken things off with Lawrence months before, Tessa had just found out about her a few days prior to her showing up at Ivy's townhouse, and she became enraged, and thus on a mission to "teach her a lesson" as she had threatened during her attack.

During Tessa's subsequent trial, it came out that Ivy had been one of many women Lawrence had omitted telling that he was married and they'd all had to deal with the wrath of Tessa after she'd found out about each of them. There were a total of six, including Ivy. The only difference between them and Ivy is that she hadn't attempted to mutilate them. Apparently, Ivy had been her breaking point.

Ivy couldn't help but to feel some sympathy for Tessa. She was a woman who thought she had married a good man, but he'd turned out to be just the opposite. Now, she'd be spending time in jail and away from their four children all because her husband couldn't honor his wedding vows. It was sad, and only confirmed what Ivy had been saying all along about marriage and why she'd never had visions of white dresses and baby rattles. It was useless. Who wanted to end up like Tessa Baxter?

Ivy's iPhone buzzed from an incoming text message, breaking her from the bad trek down memory lane. It was Kean.

Looking forward to seeing you, pretty lady.

Ivy felt bad because she was going to have to cancel. They'd made plans for a brief getaway to the North Carolina coast and were going to stay at her family's beach house. He was planning to fly in late that Friday afternoon and they were going to make the drive to get there by that evening.

Ivy loved that beach house, and it would be the perfect reprieve from life in Charlotte right now. She had a myriad of great memories from childhood to the present of spending time there with her family, which was a tradition they'd kept even after their parents passed away. They'd purchased the property right after Bridgette was born, and now, Ivy and her sisters co-owned it. They had done some major remodeling a few years ago, each adding their own personal touches to it while bickering through the entire process, but it had turned out beautiful. Ivy had looked forward to spending time there with Kean, if only briefly, but now, she wouldn't be able to. She had to be around for her sisters. She hoped he'd understand.

Chapter Thirty

"I got here as soon as I could once I received Savannah's message," Julius said, hugging Ivy and then joining her at the table she was sitting at. He'd texted her when he hadn't been able to reach Savannah. "I explained to the judge that I had a family emergency, so Winston will continue on without me today."

"I'm sure it'll comfort Savannah to see you," said Ivy. She noticed the worry lines etched in his face, and she knew learning of Bridgette's miscarriage had to be just as hard on him as well.

"How is she?" he asked.

"Not too good. There was a little altercation."

Julius frowned. "With who? Bridgette?"

Ivy shook her head. "No. Nick. And it got ugly."

Julius stared at Ivy in bewilderment as she relayed to him what happened between his wife and brother-in-law.

"I regret I wasn't here to prevent that. I feel like I should call Nick to apologize. It's obvious Savannah is stressed over this because she would never behave that way otherwise," said Julius.

"I know. It took me by surprise too, but she's been through so much and I guess this was just one more thing that sent her over the edge. We all have our breaking points," said Ivy, finishing off the remains of her bottled water.

"True. I hope Bridgette will be okay. I know how much she wanted to do this for us."

"I know my sister, and she's going to blame herself because she always feels like she has to be responsible for everyone," said Ivy.

"You're probably right, but she shouldn't. It's just unfortunate, but things happen," Julius lamented.

Ivy could hear the sadness in his voice. "How are you feeling about all of this, brother-in-law? It was your baby as well."

He shrugged. "It sucks, but I'm more concerned about Savannah and how she's going to handle it. I'm afraid she'll sink back into a depression, and I certainly don't want that to happen."

"I understand. I'm worried how this will affect both of my sisters. Like you said, it's an unfortunate situation," said Ivy, running her fingers through the soft curls of her short, pixie-cut hairstyle.

They both sat silently for a few minutes both in their own thoughts.

"I haven't told anyone just yet, and you're the first, but I received a call from my agent a few days ago for an opportunity to work on the set of a new movie directed by Ava DuVernay. But, considering everything that has just happened I think I'm going to turn it down," said Ivy, breaking their silence.

"Wow, Ivy. That's pretty major. Are you sure you want to do that?"

"I don't think I have a choice right now. I can't take off somewhere for another couple months when my sisters are both dealing with such tragic losses. I feel like I need to be here for the both of them."

"I'm sure they both would love that," said Julius.

As much as Ivy had been looking forward to working with one of her idols, her sisters were now her priority. She couldn't believe it herself that she was even considering turning down such an opportunity because up until today, she wouldn't have given it a second thought. Good money was always her first choice, but as she was learning, it wasn't everything—her family was though.

∞

Savannah rushed into her husband's arms when she saw him and Ivy in the waiting area after her treatment was complete. She'd been a complete mess the entire time, crying on and off and causing great concern for her radiation therapist. It had to be one of the worst, miserable times of her life. She couldn't help thinking what she had done to deserve all the terrible things that had been happening to her lately, despite hearing her mother's voice warning her against such negative thoughts.

"It's okay, baby," Julius whispered as she buried her face into his chest. She didn't care that people were looking at them. He led her out of the waiting area and away from the curious stares with Ivy following close behind them. When they reached a more private area of the hospital in a sitting area, they sat down next to each other on a couch. Ivy excused herself to go make a call to give them some alone time.

"I really wanted this baby for us, Julius," Savannah said, gazing at her husband through tear-filled eyes. Julius swiped her tears with his thumb, but they kept coming.

"I know, sweetheart. We both did, but we can still be parents. There are plenty of children who need good homes. That's something we can always consider in the future," said Julius.

"Would you really be satisfied with raising someone else's child?" Savannah asked because she didn't think she would be as much as she loved children.

"I know I could, and I'm certain you could too. Think about all of those little faces you're surrounded by daily, and imagine them in need of someone to love and take care of them. You would do it without hesitation," said Julius. "That's who you are and why you chose the profession you're in."

Savannah pondered her husband's words, but she just wasn't as convinced as he seemed to be, and she felt disgusted with herself for her selfish thoughts, especially as an educator of young children. But, it didn't change how she felt deep down inside—she would always want a natural child, and that brought more tears to her eyes because that chance had been snatched away from her—again.

Chapter Thirty-One

A few hours later, flowers surrounded Bridgette, and normally, she loved them. Her favorites were calla lilies and peonies. Her mother used to always say that flowers should be enjoyed while we're living, but today, she hated the sight of them. She felt like she was in a funeral home, and they made her feel dead inside. She wanted them gone. They were too much of a reminder of her loss. She summoned the nurse into her room.

"Is everything okay, Mrs. Harper? Are you feeling any pain?" the young, blonde nurse asked her when she entered the room and approached her bed.

"No, but I'd like these flowers removed," Bridgette said, glancing toward the colorful arrangements that lined both sides of the wall. There had to be well over two-dozen flowers. Some from her staff, sorority sisters and friends, but most of them had been from Nick. Bridgette was sure it was his feeble attempt at trying to ease his guilt. But, it was an epic fail. As her husband, his treatment of her had been deplorable and she didn't know if she'd ever be able to get past it.

"Are you having some sort of a reaction to them?" she asked.

Bridgette shook her head, even though it probably appeared that way since her eyes were still red and puffy from crying.

"No. I just don't want them in here anymore," Bridgette said.

The nurse glanced around the room. "They're beautiful," she mused.

"Well, you're welcome to as many of them as you want. But, please just get them out of here," Bridgette said.

The nurse gave her a sympathetic smile. "I'll send some of the volunteers in here to remove them," she said.

"Thank you."

The nurse smiled at her one last time before leaving. Ten minutes later, two hospital volunteers came in and began removing the flowers when Savannah and Julius along with Ivy who was carrying another large bouquet entered the room.

"What's going on here?" Ivy asked with a deep frown, sitting her bouquet down on one of the now empty tables.

"I feel like I'm suffocating with all of these flowers," said Bridgette. Her eyes filled up with tears again at the sight of her family. She was glad to see them. She'd felt alone, especially after Fatima had left. And, she was missing her children terribly. Her eyes focused on Savannah, praying that she didn't hate her. And when, Savannah rushed over and hugged her she couldn't hold back her sobs.

The two sisters held onto each other as if their lives depended on it. Both of them crying, bound by their loss.

Ivy and Julius stood back, giving them their much-needed moment as tears filled Ivy's eyes.

"I'm so sorry, Savannah," Bridgette cried. Her voice was barely audible amongst both of their sobs.

"It's not your fault, Bridgette. You tried and I know how much you wanted to have this baby for us, and for that I'll always be grateful. I'd never blame you. You're my big sister, and I love you so much," Savannah cried.

Ivy finally joined her sisters at the bed and wrapped her arms around them in a group hug.

"We're going to get through this, sissies," Ivy whispered.

"I love you, Ivy. And, I'm sorry. For everything," Bridgette said.

"Me too, Bre Bre," Ivy responded.

Bridgette knew they had a lot of work to do as a sisterhood, but their sisterly love was a bond that nothing could infiltrate. Not distance, not disease, not arguments or tragic losses, and they'd endured them all. If anything, it always made them stronger.

Chapter Thirty-Two

Savannah and Ivy sat on either side of Bridgette's hospital bed as they all ate dinner from Bojangles' Chicken that Julius had gone out to get them because Ivy said she was starving and she refused to eat any more food from the cafeteria. Julius stayed briefly, but felt they needed their sister time together, which they appreciated. Bridgette was thankful that he'd come to visit her and offer his support, letting her know that he didn't blame her either. She felt a little better hearing him and Savannah say that, even though she would always feel some guilt.

They were watching TV, and Bridgette decided to inquire about the altercation they'd had earlier with Nick. It was nagging at her.

"So, when will one of you tell me what happened out there earlier? Fatima was here and we heard you," Bridgette asked, looking from one sister to the other.

Savannah glanced at Ivy, and Ivy gave her a look as if to say, "You tell her". It reminded Bridgette of when they were younger, and their mother would catch the two of them doing something they weren't supposed to. They both wore the same guilty expressions.

"That was your baby sister over there acting like she was Floyd Mayweather," said Ivy, biting into a chicken drumstick.

"What? Savannah did you hit my husband?" Bridgette asked.

Savannah glared at Ivy. "You can't keep your mouth shut about anything, can you?"

"Savannah Leah, I know you didn't? You're in no condition to be behaving that way," Bridgette admonished.

"Ain't that the pot calling the kettle? Didn't you do the same thing?" Ivy asked Bridgette.

"Well, that's beside the point. That's my husband, not hers. How would you feel if I hit Julius?"

"Julius wouldn't treat me like Nick has been treating you. He's the reason you're here. And why—," Savannah dropped the piece of fried chicken she'd been eating onto the plate in her hand and sprung to her feet, placing it in her chair as she hurried to the adjoining bathroom with her hand over her mouth.

A few seconds later, they heard her vomiting. Ivy sat her plate down and went to check on her. Shortly thereafter, both sisters retreated from the bathroom. Ivy wet a paper towel in the small sink next to the bathroom door and handed it to Savannah who used it to wipe her mouth.

"Are you okay?" Bridgette asked. Her momentary anger with her baby sister for slapping her husband dissipated. Savannah's fragile appearance softened her stance. While she didn't approve of what she'd done, she understood it because she'd been in her position hours earlier, feeling frustrated and emotional. Savannah had lost the most out of all of them, and she had every right to feel however she felt. Who could really blame her? She was enduring so many battles. And Bridgette couldn't help but to feel responsible for adding yet another.

"I will be," Savannah murmured. "Ivy, I'm ready to go home, now. It's been a long day and I'm starting to feel tired."

Ivy placed a hand on her back. "Sure, sweetie," she replied. "Do you need anything before we leave, Bridge?"

Bridgette shook her head. "I'm fine. I'll probably start one of these books you bought me from the gift shop," Bridgette motioned to three novels stacked on the bedside table, "and then try to get some rest myself. I don't know how well I'll sleep in here, though." She was glad she was being discharged the next day.

"I tell you what? I'll take Savannah home, make sure she's settled in and then, I'll come back here and stay with you tonight," Ivy said.

Bridgette smiled. It was definitely a new experience to see Ivy stepping into the supportive sister role since Bridgette had been doing it for most of their lives. But, she appreciated it.

"You don't have to do that. I'd feel much better if you look after Savannah," said Bridgette, glancing at her baby sister and feeling saddened by how vulnerable she looked.

"I'll be fine once I get home. You won't have to stay and look after me. Julius will be there," said Savannah.

"I'll just stay one more night. Julius will just have to deal with it," said Ivy, grabbing her purse from a table and swinging it onto her shoulder. She walked over and kissed Bridgette on the cheek. "I'll be back tomorrow to pick you up. Get some rest. Love you."

Both of her sisters were now at her bedside with hugs and kisses.

"Love you, sissies. Thanks so much for coming. Savannah, you try to get some rest as well. Okay?" Bridgette said.

Savannah gave her a weak smile.

Bridgette could tell she wasn't feeling well. She was glad Savannah was finally done with her cancer treatments. She watched them leave, as Ivy escorted Savannah out with her arm around her shoulder for support. The gesture touched Bridgette because it just reminded her of how much they were always there for each other when they needed it the most. She had to admit, it was strange not having Nick there. A part of her wanted him to be. He was still her husband, regardless if they were having issues. She wanted the life she had before everything started to fall apart.

Chapter Thirty-Three

Ivy heard wailing from the guest bedroom where she had been sleeping and hopped out of bed to investigate the source. It was coming from Savannah's baby nursery down the hall. Ivy rushed towards the cries, her bare feet suddenly feeling like lead against the cool hardwood floor as she got closer. When she finally got to the door and turned the knob, her heart clenched at the sight before her.

"Oh. My. God. Savannah, what happened?" Ivy screamed as she ran and knelt down on the plush carpet next to her sister who was surrounded by a pool of blood and lying in a fetal position. Ivy gingerly turned her over on her back as Savannah gasped for air. She was suffocating from her own blood that was seeping through her silk, nightgown from her stomach.

"Oh. My. God. Oh. My God," Ivy yelled repeatedly, her tears blinding her. "Hang on, sis. You can't die on me. Julius," she screamed.

"He can't help you. He's dead. And you're next," said the icy voice behind her, causing Ivy's own blood to run cold. She turned her head slowly as her eyes locked with a set of steely, distant ones she thought she'd never see again; At least not in eight more years.

"Tessa?" Ivy uttered in shock at the woman who'd traumatized her two years ago on that cold November evening.

"I told you I was going to finish what I started," she threatened and Ivy noticed the box cutter dripping with blood clutched in her hand as she lunged toward her.

Ivy let out a bloodcurdling yelp as Tessa raised the deadly weapon over her, plunging it at her face.

Ivy shot up in bed covered in a cold sweat and slightly panting. She hadn't had a nightmare in a while, at least in the last six months, but they were often brought on by added stress. And Tessa Baxter was always the antagonist in these nightmares, threatening to finish what she started, but this one unnerved her because this was the first time that it had involved her family. Maybe it was because she was staying the night at Savannah and Julius's.

She grabbed her iPhone off the nightstand to see what time it was. It was 1:58. She'd gone to bed only two hours ago. She hated that she was out of her Ambien prescription, but hadn't had time to fill it because it's what helped her sleep through the night most of the time. She'd have to do it ASAP. Ivy placed her phone back on the nightstand before hopping out of bed to head to the adjoining bathroom to splash her face with cold water.

After retreating from the bathroom, she decided to get something to drink and headed downstairs to the kitchen for some water, but her steps slowed down at the soft cries she heard coming from the baby's nursery down the hall. Ivy had an eerie feeling of déjà vu as her heart rate quickened. She walked slowly toward the sound and when she reached the door and turned the knob she saw Savannah balled up in a fetal position on the carpet, clutching a stuffed animal to her stomach.

"Savannah?" Ivy mumbled as she rushed over and kneeled down next to her sister.

"My baby," Savannah sobbed.

"I know, sweetie. I know it hurts," Ivy said, rubbing her arm. She lay down next to her sister, her face close to hers as she wrapped an arm around her, comforting her while she released her sorrow. Ivy couldn't help but to cry with her because her sister's pain was so palpable. It reminded her of when they were younger, and Savannah got scared after having a nightmare from staying up late to sneak and watch scary movies, something they weren't allowed to watch at eight and ten years old, and she'd climb into Ivy's bed and sleep under her the remainder of the night.

In that moment as her sister mourned the loss of her unborn baby, Ivy knew she had made the right decision to turn down working on that Ava DuVernay movie. This was where she needed to be.

Chapter Thirty-Four

Bridgette was glad to be home from the hospital the following Saturday and with her boys as they sat huddled together in the family room watching the Disney movie, *Frozen*. They didn't seem to want to let her out of their sight, and Bridgette hated that they felt that way. She knew how frightened they'd been when she'd had to go to the hospital and hadn't returned home that day. She explained to them that she hadn't been feeling well and that the doctor wanted to make sure she was okay, so that's why she couldn't come home, purposely omitting the fact that she was pregnant and lost the baby. She felt like it would be too much for them to process, and debated if she would even tell them in the future. She didn't know what purpose it would serve since they didn't know she'd been pregnant in the first place.

She heard the chime of the doorbell and Dylan raced out of the room towards the foyer to answer the door. He walked back into the family room with Ivy in tow, carrying two large boxes of pizza.

"Auntie Ivy brought pizza from Mellow Mushroom, Mom," Dylan said with excitement. Bridgette smiled at her sister.

"I know, sweetheart. She wanted to surprise you guys. You and Ryan take them into the kitchen. And make sure you wash your hands before opening those boxes," said Bridgette.

"Did you get pepperoni, Auntie Ivy?" Ryan inquired.

"Of course, I did, Ry-Ry," said Ivy; referring to her youngest nephew by the nickname she'd been calling him since he was a baby. "And just plain cheese for Dylan." She handed a box to each boy.

"Thank you, Auntie Ivy," Dylan exclaimed.

"Yeah. Thanks, Auntie Ivy," Ryan repeated after his twin brother. Both boys hurried out of the room to enjoy their pizza, the movie they'd been watching with their mother, now a second thought.

"How you doing, sissy?" Ivy asked. She leaned down and placed a kiss on Bridgette's cheek and then sat next to her on the sectional.

"I'm okay. Just glad to be home. I love those boots," said Bridgette, pointing to the thigh-high, brown, suede, wedge boots Ivy was sporting with a pair of fitted, dark blue jeans and a crème-colored sweater.

"Thanks, sis. You know how much I love the fall season, and being able to break out my boots."

"I love this time of the year too. It'll be time to take the boys to the state fair soon. They always enjoy themselves and manage to wear Nick and I out in the process," Bridgette chuckled.

"Where is he?" Ivy asked.

"I have no clue. I haven't been able to look at him since I've been home."

"Has he tried talking to you about what happened?" Ivy asked, bending to unzip her boots.

"He's apologized, but I don't feel it's genuine. I just think he's feeling guilty about how he's treated me and let Cassietta fill his head with a bunch of nonsense. I'd been trying to get him to talk to me so we could try to work out our issues, but he always brushed me off and pretty much gave me his backside to kiss. So, I'm at an impasse right now on how to move forward with this marriage," Bridgette lamented.

"I really hate to hear that. I think he has his faults like we all do, but I don't think it's anything you two can't get past. I know how much he loves you and the boys." Ivy removed her boots and then got comfortable on the sectional, propping her feet up behind her.

"I'm going to pray about it because that's all I've got right now. What's been going on with you?" Bridgette asked, eager to change the subject.

"Well, I debated if I was going to even mention this, but I got an offer to work with Ava DuVernay on the set of a new movie she's directing next month in Toronto," said Ivy.

"Ivy, that's wonderful. I know how much you love her work. Why wouldn't you mention it?"

"Because I turned it down. I called my agent this morning and told him I couldn't accept this time."

"Why would you do that? That's like one of your dream jobs," Bridgette queried, looking at her sister with confusion.

"I need to be here in Charlotte with you and Savannah. There's no way I'm running off again and leaving you two after what you've both been through," said Ivy.

Bridgette couldn't believe what her sister was saying. She was truly dumbfounded.

"Who are you and what have you done with my sister?" she asked, making Ivy chuckle.

"There's something else I want to talk to you about also," said Ivy. She had a nervous look on her face that Bridgette had never seen before.

"What's up? And what's that look about? And please don't tell me something crazy like you're getting married. I might pass out right here, and I'm not trying to end back up in the hospital," Bridgette joked.

"Girl, bye. It's definitely not that," said Ivy, waving a hand in dismissal like that was the most ridiculous thing her sister could say.

"Okay. I was about to say. Not that it would be a bad thing, but I'd probably go into shock."

"Well…you might want to hear me out first," said Ivy, gazing at her sister with uncertainty.

"I hope you're going to tell me some time today and stop torturing me," Bridgette said.

Ivy took a deep breath. "What do you think about me being Savannah's surrogate?"

"Huh?" Bridgette had an incredulous look on her face.

"I've been thinking about it and it's been weighing on my mind heavily," said Ivy.

"Ivy, where is this coming from? Do you have any idea what you're saying? This isn't a game. You can't play with people's lives," Bridgette balked and Ivy frowned. It was obvious she wasn't expecting Bridgette to react the way she did, but it was the most ludicrous thing she'd ever heard Ivy say, and there had been many.

"Who said that I was playing? I've never been more serious about anything in my life."

Bridgette could tell she'd hurt her sister's feelings by the pained expression she was wearing. She remained silent, haunted by Ivy's last statement because she'd said those very words to Nick, and he'd made her feel the same way Ivy was.

"Why do you want to do this?" Bridgette asked after a few minutes of silence passed. "It's not easy. You'll have to sacrifice so much, Ivy. I'm not sure you know what you'll be getting yourself into."

"You're right, sis. I don't know, but I want to try. We've both seen our dreams come into fruition. You've opened a successful bakery that you always talked about doing and I've travelled the world, working with some of the most influential people while doing what I love and always dreamed about. Don't you think it's time for Savannah to see her dream finally realized?" Ivy asked.

Her words brought tears to Bridgette's eyes because she had never thought about it that way. Her reasoning had always come from a maternal instinct; a bond she'd always shared with Savannah.

Bridgette took her sister's hand and gently squeezed it. It was not only a gesture of approval, but finally—of solidarity.

"I'll be here for you every step of the way."

Chapter Thirty-Five

Ivy had never been more nervous about anything in her life. She'd been going back and forth in her mind about being Savannah's surrogate, and questioning if she was doing the right thing. And she knew that once she said those words to her sister, there would be no taking them back. She'd vomited in the toilet twice before Bridgette had showed up at her condo the following Sunday morning to pick her up. She was going to go with Ivy to Savannah and Julius's to support her in talking with them. She was grateful that Bridgette had decided to forgo church service that morning, something she never did because Ivy didn't know if she could do it alone.

"Everything will be fine, Ivy. Now, they may be a little shocked as I was, but at least you would've put it out there for them to consider. I'm really proud of you for doing this," said Bridgette, smiling at Ivy as they rode in her Suburban.

"We'll see how it all goes," said Ivy with uncertainty.

Just then, one of their mother's favorite gospel songs came on the Sirius XM satellite gospel station Bridgette always listened to and they looked at each other and smiled. Ivy knew Bridgette was thinking what she was thinking—it was a sign.

Ivy began singing the lyrics to "Expect Your Miracle" by The Clark Sisters with Bridgette joining along.

"I'm looking for a miracle. I expect the impossible. I live the intangible. I see the invisible," they sang.

❧

Ivy and Bridgette stood on their youngest sister's front porch, holding hands. They were forehead to forehead, both with their eyes closed while Bridgette recited a prayer.

"In Jesus name we pray. Amen," Bridgette said, after she was done.

"Amen," Ivy repeated. "Okay, I think I'm ready now," she said when they released their hands.

Bridgette winked at her. "You've got this."

Ivy pressed the doorbell, and a few seconds later, Julius appeared at the front door.

"Good morning, sisters," he said, ushering them into the foyer and placing kisses on both of their cheeks.

"Good morning," Ivy and Bridgette replied in unison.

"Do I smell bacon?" Ivy inquired, removing her leather jacket and hanging it on a hook.

"Yup. Just got finished whipping up a Chef Yancey breakfast special," said Julius.

"Well, we appreciate that. Where's Savannah?" Bridgette asked.

"She's still lying down. I told her I'd let her know when y'all got here."

Fifteen minutes later, they were all seated in the breakfast nook that also offered a beautiful view of Lake Norman. Julius had made a delicious spread of bacon, scrambled eggs, cheese grits and hash brown casserole along with mixed fruit and wheat toast.

"So, what did you want to talk to us about?" Julius asked, looking at Ivy.

Ivy glanced at Bridgette seated next to her who gave her a nod, and then she looked at Savannah who'd been noticeably quiet and picking at her food. Ivy could tell she was still going through it emotionally, and she had dark circles under her eyes as if she hadn't been sleeping.

Ivy hadn't been able to stop thinking about that awful nightmare she'd had and then seeing her sister having a breakdown. It had brought everything into perspective for her.

"Well, I know this is going to seem a little odd, especially coming from me," Ivy chuckled, trying to ease the anxiety she felt. "But, it's not something I take lightly, so don't laugh in my face when I say this."

Now, all eyes were on her and she took a deep breath. She looked at Savannah who was sitting directly across from her, and her eyes seemed empty. It tugged at her heart that her sister was becoming a shell of the woman she once was before cervical cancer had infiltrated her body. She looked from Savannah and then to Julius.

"What would you guys think about me being your surrogate?" she finally said, and then felt like a weight had been lifted from her because she'd finally gotten it out.

Savannah burst into tears, surprising them all. Julius immediately pulled her close to him to comfort her.

"I'm sorry, sis if I upset you," said Ivy, feeling horrible. This is what she'd been afraid of. Maybe it was too soon. It had only been a few days since Bridgette's miscarriage.

"We know you're trying to help, Ivy and we appreciate it, but—," Julius began. Savannah hopped out of her seat, cutting him off as she rushed to Ivy and threw her arms around her as she sobbed. She didn't have to say anything because her tears were her answer.

☙

Am I really going to do this? Ivy thought, a few hours later as she sat on the floor of Savannah's baby nursery where she'd found her crying nights earlier. She was still pondering her decision after the fact.

"I think I should change the theme of the nursery. New baby. New journey," Savannah lamented, sitting in the white rocking chair she'd been thrilled about finally finding, breaking Ivy out of her thoughts.

"I love this safari theme. It's pretty baby neutral," said Bridgette, surveying the room. She was sitting a few feet away from Ivy.

"Maybe I'm being superstitious. I'm still in shock. I guess," she chuckled. "I would've never, ever in a million years thought I'd be saying Ivy and baby in the same sentence."

That makes two of us, Ivy thought, laughing with her sisters because when she thought about it, it was kind of funny considering her stance on motherhood. And she didn't want anyone to get it twisted because she still felt that way. She was just doing her sister a favor and basically renting her uterus out to her. That was it.

"You never know. This could be the catalyst for future babies," said Bridgette, looking at Ivy.

"Girl, boo," said Ivy. "Once that nine-month stint is over. It'll be back to grinding for me."

"Don't rule it out. God sometimes has a funny sense of humor. This situation is certainly a good example," said Bridgette.

"I agree, sis. Maybe even a hubby too," Savannah quipped.

"Now, y'all are talking crazy," said Ivy. And then, her mind flashed to Kean.

Oh my God. Kean. How am I going to explain this to him? She thought.

With everything that had been going on, she hadn't thought about how he would fit into her decision. There was no way she could continue to see him, especially if she ended up pregnant. He would become tabloid fodder with his celebrity status, and they'd done a good job so far of staying out of them.

As her sisters continued trying to predict her future, she excused herself saying she needed to return a call to a client. A few minutes later, she had her iPhone in her hand. She had to get this over with while she still had the nerve. It was best to do it sooner rather than later. She hated to though because she'd really grown to like Kean—a lot. But again, her family had to come first.

Hey. I'll be off the grid for a while. Family stuff, she typed.

Everything okay? He replied.

It will be. Just wanted to let you know because I won't be able to see you. Too much going on right now.

L Sorry to hear that. Thought we were going somewhere with this. I guess I understand though. Family first.

Thanks for understanding. Take care, she typed. She really felt terrible, but it was just easier this way.

Chapter Thirty-Six

Eight months later...

Ivy rolled her eyes as she listened to her sisters' baby chatter like she wasn't sitting there at the table with them and she was getting a headache. They were having lunch at P.F. Chang's in downtown Atlanta after doing some Saturday afternoon shopping. Savannah and Bridgette had driven in from Charlotte and arrived late yesterday evening, something they'd been doing over the past few months. And while Ivy loved her sisters dearly, she'd grown tired of these visits. She always felt like they were just there to scrutinize her every move rather than spend quality time as sisters.

While they'd grown closer as the threesome they used to be before all of the turmoil months prior, their relationship had gotten a little more complicated because now, Ivy was the sister surrogate. And even though she was six months pregnant and showing, it was still hard for all of them to fathom.

"Ivy, shouldn't you be drinking more water?" Savannah asked, eyeing the glass of sweet iced tea the waitress had just sat in front of her.

"I drink plenty of water," Ivy responded, picking up her glass and taking a sip out of her straw.

"I'm just saying. That's like your third glass of sweet tea."

"And?" Ivy asked with annoyance. "It's better than the glass of red wine I'd prefer to have right now."

"All of that sugar isn't good for the baby," said Savannah in the condescending tone that Ivy had grown to detest. It was like Savannah had switched places with Bridgette and that wasn't a good thing.

"It's not that sweet, Savannah. It's fine," Ivy rebuffed.

" I'm not trying to tell you what to do. I just want to make sure you're taking care of yourself."

"You mean taking care of *your* baby," Ivy retorted. "Don't worry. I won't do anything to damage your precious cargo."

"That's not what I meant at all. Relax." Savannah shook her head in frustration.

Ivy rolled her eyes and eased out of her seat. "Excuse me. I have to go to the bathroom," she said and walked off in that direction.

As she made her way to her destination, she slowed down at the sight of the familiar face staring at her with a look of confusion. She wanted to turn and run in the other direction, but the way the baby was sitting on her bladder she had to get to the bathroom and this was the only path there. She had no choice.

"Ivy?" the familiar face said, as she got closer.

Ivy plastered on a smile despite her insides feeling like Jell-O. She hadn't seen him in a while, not since she'd abruptly ended their on again-off again relationship.

"Hello, Kean. How are you?" she asked. First, taking notice of how handsome he still was, and then of the woman sitting at the table with him. There was also a young girl there who resembled Kean, except for her golden, pecan tan complexion compared to his dark chocolate one. She had to be his daughter, Marley who Ivy had never got the chance to officially meet. Ivy greeted them both with a smile.

"Great, but I should ask you the same," he said, his eyes resting on her baby bump.

She placed a hand on her growing mound. The way he was looking at her made Ivy want to crawl under one of the tables. She was sure her pregnancy was alarming to him.

"I'm doing well. And this beautiful, young lady must be your daughter. She looks just like you," she said, changing the subject.

The little girl giggled and Ivy could see that she was in the snaggle-toothed stage of childhood with her missing front teeth. She was sitting next to Kean, munching on a spring roll.

"Yup. This is my Marley Marl," he said, nudging the girl with his elbow playfully, causing her to giggle again.

The woman beamed at them from across the table, as she sipped from a glass of water. Something about the pride that gleamed from her eyes, made Ivy envious. Like they were a family.

"And, this is Octavia. Marley's mother," Kean introduced them, confirming what Ivy already surmised.

The women acknowledged each other with pleasant smiles.

"It's nice to meet you. Both of you," Ivy said, looking from mother and then to daughter. "And, I love your hair.

The color really is stunning." Ivy complimented Octavia who had an intriguing, natural mane of reddish brown hair that accentuated her latte complexion. She could also tell from her stylish attire that she was a fashionista like Ivy was. They could probably have been friends under different circumstances.

"Oh, thank you. I love your curly, pixie cut as well," she said.

Ivy smiled and thanked her.

"Well, it was good seeing you again, Kean. You all enjoy your lunch," Ivy said, smiling one last time before walking off. She couldn't get to the bathroom and away from Kean's questioning stare fast enough. She didn't realize how much she missed him until that moment.

This whole pregnancy thing was still something she was adjusting to, and it hadn't been easy. Ivy faced challenges from the very beginning, starting with the in vitro fertilization. Dr. Billingsley, Savannah's fertility specialist had been concerned with the fact that Ivy had never given birth before, a requirement of hers that she was usually unwavering on since there were risks that could potentially compromise her own fertility in the future, and also how it could affect her emotionally. But after Ivy went through the psychological evaluation and they were satisfied that she was equipped to endure the process, she was finally cleared. Then, there had been the how many embryos to transfer dilemma, which was a point of contention between she and Savannah.

Savannah wanted to transfer two like they'd done with Bridgette to increase their chances, but Ivy had refused to do it. She was only going to allow one, and if Savannah couldn't accept that then she'd have to find someone else. Ivy hated to give her that ultimatum, but there was no way she was going to risk getting pregnant with twins. She loved her body too much for that, and she wanted to be able to bounce right back after giving birth. Savannah relented, but she didn't speak to Ivy for a week after. It had all been enough to make her want to drink, but that hadn't been an option—unfortunately.

Chapter Thirty-Seven

Savannah's frustration with Ivy was growing with her pregnancy. While she was beyond grateful that Ivy had agreed to carry her baby and this was more than likely her last hope for a natural child, she couldn't help but to feel anxious for it to be over. The two of them were bickering constantly to the point where she was getting headaches on a regular basis. Ivy was always combative when she suggested something regarding her pregnancy, and she hardly answered her calls when she wanted updates after her doctor's appointments. She hated the fact that Ivy wasn't in Charlotte and chose to stay in Atlanta because she would've liked to be more involved in the day-to-day of her pregnancy.

As she watched her sister ease from her seat to make one of her frequent trips to the bathroom, there was something else that she hated to admit and it started when Ivy really began showing—she was feeling envious. Her sister was always a beautiful woman, but pregnancy seemed to enhance it. Ivy had that glow that she'd seen many pregnant women radiate, and since she and Ivy were close in age, just two years apart and closely resembled each other, Savannah often wondered if she would have looked similar if she could carry a baby.

"What's wrong, Savannah?" Bridgette asked, snapping her out of her thoughts.

"Nothing," she said curtly, picking up her water glass and taking a sip from the straw.

"Well, that didn't sound like nothing. What's up?"

Savannah deep sighed. "Ivy is really working my nerves is all, but it'll be fine. I guess."

"And it will be. Emotions are all over the place right now, and that's to be expected. You only have a few more months to go, so hang in there," said Bridgette, smiling.

"Thank God," Savannah muttered, causing Bridgette to chuckle.

"It's not that bad. Remember how I was when I was pregnant with the boys during those last few months. Ivy seems like a saint compared to me."

"I wouldn't go that far, but I did feel bad for Nick. *Then*," said Savannah.

She was still salty with her brother-in-law months later after Bridgette's miscarriage, but out of respect for her big sister, she refrained from making any outright nasty comments about him because she knew Bridgette was still struggling about her marriage. And she did still feel a little responsible for their discord. Her want for a baby had seemed to cause a lot of family drama, and she really didn't understand why. In her opinion, a baby was a blessing, so if anything it should have brought them all together, but that certainly hadn't happened.

"Have you narrowed down the baby names yet?" asked Bridgette, ignoring her dig at her husband and scooping brown rice into her mouth.

Savannah shook her head. "It's kind of hard since we don't know the sex of the baby just yet, but I'm looking forward to the gender reveal at the upcoming baby shower."

"I am too. And I'm honored that you're going to let me be the one to do it," Bridgette said with a proud smile after swallowing her food and wiping her mouth with her cloth napkin.

"I'm excited," Savannah beamed. They'd had the ultrasound technician to seal the information of the baby's sex in an envelope over a month ago, and they'd given it to Bridgette for safekeeping until the baby shower, which they were having in a few weeks.

Savannah still couldn't believe that she was going to be a mother in three more months provided Ivy continued to do what she was supposed to do.

Chapter Thirty-Eight

After church and then having brunch the following Sunday, Ivy bid her sisters farewell and safe travels as they got on the road headed back to North Carolina, but not before her and Savannah got into another spat about taking care of herself, which was code talk for taking care of the baby. Savannah worried about everything, and Ivy definitely understood why, but it didn't mean that it wasn't annoying and a bit insulting. Ivy didn't need to be counseled on every aspect of her pregnancy. She'd done a pretty good job thus far, considering she'd gotten further along than Bridgette had. But, she'd never be so insensitive as to say that out loud, even though she'd thought it.

She knew Savannah was beyond grateful and thankful because she said it all the time, but it was almost as if she didn't trust Ivy to be responsible enough to ensure that she had a healthy pregnancy. She'd even suggested Ivy move back to Charlotte a few weeks after learning of her pregnancy because she wanted to "keep a close watch" on her and Ivy balked at the suggestion. Ivy was surprised at all of Bridgette's bad traits that Savannah had seemed to be picking up and she confronted Bridgette thinking she was behind it.

"Bridgette, have you been in Savannah's ear?" Ivy queried.

"No. Why are you asking me that?"

"Because a lot of what comes out of your baby sister's mouth lately sounds too much like you," Ivy retorted.

Bridgette chuckled. "I don't know if I should be insulted or not, but okay. What's going on?"

"Savannah has it in her mind that she needs to keep an eye on me. I haven't had anybody do that since Mama and Daddy, and that's where it ended. I'm a grown woman. I can take care of myself and I'm capable of taking care of someone else for that matter," Ivy said, placing a hand on her belly that would soon have a bulge.

"She doesn't mean it that way, Ivy. She's just worried since…" Bridgette's words trailed off.

Ivy knew it was still hard for her to talk about the miscarriage. It was for all of them.

"I know. But, I can't go through the next nine months having her trying to police my every move. I'm doing this for her and for no other reason, so she has to relax," Ivy complained. "I mean, I'm only a few weeks into this pregnancy and she's already acting like a prison warden. I. Can't."

Bridgette chuckled again. "She was the same with me to a certain extent, but she knew that I was already experienced in it. But, that still didn't matter in the end," Bridgette lamented and Ivy could hear the guilt and sadness in her voice.

"Don't go there, sissy. You have to stop blaming yourself. It matters because you tried and if it weren't for you, I wouldn't have even considered being Savannah's surrogate. So, see there's always a blessing to come out of everything," Ivy said.

"Wow, you sounded just like Mama when you said that," said Bridgette, *which made Ivy smile from the inside out. That was the biggest compliment her big sister could ever give her.*

"Well, she's always around us so I'm not surprised," said Ivy.

"I agree. She's definitely been with me and I know that because I haven't ended up in a mental ward or jail for that matter," said Bridgette, *and Ivy knew she was referring to her souring marriage.*

"Amen," said Ivy.

A sharp movement in her stomach brought Ivy out of her thoughts as she sat in her living room, propped up on the sofa, flipping through the latest issue of *In Style* magazine.

"Oh my," she exclaimed, placing a hand on her protruding belly. And then, it happened again. It was the first time Ivy had felt the baby kick, and it was a little jarring, but she was amused by it.

"You're going to be a strong, little diva like your auntie." Ivy giggled, pressing her hand gently into her stomach.

Savannah and Julius had agreed they'd wait until the baby shower to learn the sex. Ivy was hoping it was a girl, since they already had two boys in the family. It would be awesome to have someone she could spoil and teach her fashion and make-up skills. That thought brought a smile to Ivy's face and she began humming a lullaby that her mother often sang to her and her sisters, hoping to get another reaction from the baby. And when another kick came a few minutes later, Ivy squealed in laughter.

Chapter Thirty-Nine

Bridgette would've never imagined she'd be considering divorce. It seemed as if she and Nick were at the point of irreconcilable differences. They'd grown into a habit of coexisting for the sake of their children and Bridgette wouldn't use them as an excuse to stay together anymore. It was time to make a decision once and for all.

It was obvious Nick felt the same because she'd found a lease agreement he'd signed for an apartment that he was supposed to be moving into in a few weeks and he hadn't mentioned one word about it. So, when he was going to give her the courtesy of telling her, Bridgette didn't know, but she would confront him about it.

And then, there was his mother.

Bridgette had banned Cassietta from coming to her house. If she didn't ever see that woman again in life, it wouldn't be a moment too soon. But, she knew how much her boys loved their grandmother and vice versa, so she would never discourage a relationship between them. So, Nick just took them to visit her in Durham on some weekends and Bridgette didn't have a problem with it, but she also warned him that Cassietta had better not speak ill of her in front of her children. She wouldn't tolerate it. His response was to glare at her and shake his head, which had become the extent of their communication lately. It was sad, but that is what it had come down to.

Bridgette sat waiting in the family room for Nick to arrive home from a swim meet. And when she heard him come in, she called for him. He seemed reluctant as he dropped his large gym bag by the entrance and looked at her.

"What's up?" he asked.

Bridgette could detect irritation in his voice as if she was the last person on Earth he wanted to talk to.

"We need to talk," she announced.

"Where are the boys?"

"They're in bed already."

"Go ahead and say what you have to say. I'm listening," said Nick.

Bridgette sighed. He was already giving her major attitude, so she knew this wasn't going to be an easy conversation, but it had to be had nonetheless.

"Can you come and sit down, please? I don't want to talk to you from all the way over there. There's been enough distance between us, don't you think?" Bridgette asked.

He didn't respond, but walked over to her, although begrudgingly, and sat a few feet away from her on the sectional. He stared at her, waiting for her to speak.

"When did you plan on telling me you were moving out? I found the lease you signed." Bridgette pulled the document tucked next to her and slid it across the chair toward him.

He glanced at it, unfazed and then looked back at her.

"The move-in date specified is only a few weeks away, Nick. Were you just going to wait until then to say anything?"

"Haven't had the time to," was all he said, matter-of-factly.

Bridgette wanted to slap him, but the last time she'd done that it had turned out bad. For her and her sister. She sighed. "What happened to us, Nick? I know we haven't had the perfect marriage by any means, but we always had an open line of communication."

He snickered. She hated when he did that. She always felt demeaned.

"I really wish you wouldn't laugh when I try to talk to you, especially about something so important. Our marriage is in shambles and I don't find anything amusing about that," Bridgette huffed. She could feel her anger rising, but she was trying to keep from erupting.

"I find it amusing that you think our communication has been open. The way I see it, it's always been about how you see things or feel they should be. It's your way or the highway. And this time, I'm choosing the latter," said Nick. The way he said the last sentence made Bridgette's heart drop. It sounded final like he was done with her and their marriage.

"What are you saying?"

"Since you've always acted like you're the man of the house, I won't stand in your way anymore. You can rule your kingdom like you want to now." His eyes were cold and his voice devoid of emotion.

Bridgette winced at his words. They were painful and cutting. She fought back tears. "Don't be insulting. Why don't you *be* a man and tell me what it is you're so bitter about. Everything I've ever done was to better our family. And I'm sorry if your ego won't let you see that," Bridgette said.

He shook his head. "What's the point? You'll hear what you want to hear and turn everything else I say around to make yourself look better. But the truth of the matter is, you've never valued me. Nothing I've ever done has been good enough for you."

"That's not true. Why would you say something so hurtful? We've been together almost eleven years now, and if I didn't value you we wouldn't have lasted this long or were you pretending to love me all of this time?" she asked, a tear finally falling from her eye. She wiped her wet cheek.

He seemed unmoved by her tears and seemed to be staring through her. It was clear to Bridgette that he was already gone emotionally and had just been waiting to make the physical transition from her life.

"I've always loved you and I always will. But, I won't be second to everything else in your life anymore. Not your business, not your sisters, and not even the boys," he said.

Bridgette didn't even want to fix her mouth to form the words "divorce" because if she was honest with herself, that's not what she wanted. Even after the way Nick had been treating her, even after showing a side of himself that she despised and never wanted to see again, and even with the distance that had their hearts and minds so out of sync with one another, she still wanted to be married to him. She still wanted to be Mrs. Nicholas Harper.

"Do you want out of this marriage?" she asked, her voice barely a whisper. She couldn't stop her tears from falling now. He stared into her eyes, and she no longer saw the man she was married to. It was like looking into the eyes of a stranger.

"Yes," he said, grabbing the lease and rising from the sectional. "And I'll talk to the boys. I want to be the one to tell them I'm leaving." And with that, he left Bridgette to grapple with his words.

Chapter Forty

Savannah debated on whether or not to call Ivy before heading to work. It was still fairly early; at least for Ivy who she knew always had the advantage of sleeping in, something she had the luxury of doing since she didn't work a normal job. Savannah was glad that she wasn't traveling as much now as she was in the beginning of the pregnancy, which had been another point of contention between them with all of the germs Ivy was exposing the baby to.

She knew Ivy had a doctor's appointment later that afternoon, and she wanted to make sure that she didn't miss it. This was why she hated that Ivy was in Georgia and she in North Carolina because she would have preferred not to get the information about the baby's progress second hand, but that's how it was and there wasn't much she could do about it. So, despite Ivy's crabby attitude, which she wanted to contribute to the pregnancy, she decided to call her. She'd worry all morning if she didn't and wouldn't be able to focus on much else.

"It's seven in the morning, Savannah. Is something wrong?" Ivy asked, sounding groggy.

Savannah was surprised that she had even answered.

"No. I'm just calling to make sure you don't forget your appointment this afternoon. I really wish I were there to go with you. You shouldn't be going through this alone. If you had listened to me and stayed in Charlotte like I wanted—,"

"Really, Savannah?" Ivy huffed, cutting her off. "You called me this early in the morning to gripe?"

"Sorry to wake you. I just wanted to make sure you remembered. That's all," Savannah said, ignoring her sister's attitude.

"Savannah, we've had this conversation more than I care to and it's really getting old. I'm more than capable of remembering a doctor's appointment," she snapped. "I'm not one of your students."

"I know that, Ivy. I'm just—," Savannah began, but Ivy cut her off again.

"You're getting on my nerves is what you're doing. I didn't offer to do this and put my life on hold just so you could be a pain in my backside every chance you get. Do you want me to end up in the same predicament as Bridgette because you can't lay off?" Ivy said, her voice going up an octave. "Because that is what's going to happen if you keep this up. And you'll have yourself to blame this time."

Savannah's face flushed from the sting of her sister's words. She knew that the pregnancy was making Ivy an emotional rollercoaster, but she was going too far. She'd never spoken so mean to her and Savannah wasn't used to it. It had always been Bridgette on the receiving end of her cutting words.

"Ivy, calm down. There's no need for you to get so upset and worked up. Considering we're paying for your medical care and it's our baby you're carrying, I don't think it's unreasonable for me to be concerned."

"No, it's my baby until it leaves my womb. And in case you forgot, I'm the one it has to rely on. Not you. All you've had to do is sit on the sidelines while I've gotten fat and watched my ankles swell," she spat, ending their call and leaving Savannah speechless.

Chapter Forty-One

Bridgette slid a tray of red velvet cupcakes, one of Sugar Rush's bestsellers into the glass display. A tap on the front door drew her attention. She was surprised to see her sister standing on the other side of the glass. She walked from behind the counter to let her in.

"What are you doing here? Did something happen?" Bridgette asked. Ivy and the baby flashed in her mind, and she prayed it wasn't anything concerning them.

"No," Savannah said, alleviating some of Bridgette's fears.

"You look upset. What's wrong?" Bridgette queried, studying her sister before locking the door behind them. She glanced down at her wristwatch. It was three minutes after eight o'clock. "And shouldn't you be at school?"

"Ivy went off on me this morning."

Savannah walked over to the display, her eyes gazing over the fresh baked goods Bridgette had just put out. Bridgette chuckled as she walked back behind the counter, sliding another tray of cupcakes inside.

"Oh girl. That's all? Welcome to my world," she said, waving her hand in dismissal. "Pregnancy has brought out a new kind of beast in Ivy. I'm just glad I'm getting to witness it because I never thought I'd be alive to see it," she added with an amused expression.

"Well, I don't like it. She's become mean-spirited, and I'm beginning to question if this was a good idea," Savannah lamented.

Bridgette peered at her. "Uh-oh. Let's go back into my office and talk. I'll make us some tea." Bridgette ushered her sister behind the counter and back into her office. A few minutes later, she joined her, handing Savannah a mug of her favorite chai tea.

"Thanks, big sissy," Savannah said, accepting the hot beverage and then taking a sip. Bridgette sat down next to her on the sofa. "You're welcome. Now, tell me what happened," she said, taking a sip from her own mug and then sitting it down on a side table.

Savannah sighed like she was carrying a heavy load. She'd been through so much in the last year, but thankfully, she was on the road to recovery. And Bridgette had no doubt that the baby's upcoming arrival had a lot to do with that.

"Ivy said some really awful things to me this morning. It felt like she was intentionally trying to hurt my feelings," said Savannah, running her hand through her short, soft curls. She was wearing her hair natural, now that it had grown back and Bridgette thought it made her and Ivy look almost like twins since she wore hers in a similar short style.

"I know her mouth can be reckless sometimes, so I can only imagine what came out of it. I'm almost afraid to hear what she said that got you so upset."

"Oh, she certainly said a mouthful, but what pierced me the most is her saying that the baby is hers while it's in her womb," said Savannah and Bridgette noticed the worried look on her face.

"I don't think she meant anything by it. Like I said before, this pregnancy is making her lips looser than normal. And you know that's always my point of contention with her." Bridgette took another sip from her mug.

Savannah looked at Bridgette with sadness in her eyes. "You don't think she would try and keep my baby, do you?"

Bridgette frowned. "Savannah, seriously? We're talking about Ivy here. She might be a walking contradiction right now, but she would never try and keep this baby for herself. Never," she said, pointedly. "She made it clear that she's only doing this for you. And I believe that wholeheartedly."

Savannah sipped her tea and remained silent. She had deep lines etched in her forehead as if she were pondering Bridgette's words.

"She doesn't want to be anybody's mother. Trust and believe," Bridgette continued.

"I just don't understand why she would choose to say something so hurtful. I don't like that she feels as if she can speak to me with such disregard just because she's carrying my baby. I won't tolerate it."

"I feel you. I'm sure she'll realize how out of order she was and apologize. If there's one person she hates to see upset. It's you," Bridgette said with a light chuckle.

"Well, she hasn't cared too much since she's always snapping at me every time I ask her anything concerning *my* baby. You never did that to me."

Bridgette patted her sister's hand. "Everything is going to be okay, sweetie. We're all on edge with what happened before, but that's to be expected," she said, referring to her miscarriage.

Savannah looked at her sister with seriousness. "Bridgette, I really want you to let go of your guilt. I know you went through so much and I really meant what I said. I don't blame you. You sacrificed too much for me to ever do that."

Savannah smiled at her and squeezed her hand. Her words and her gesture warmed Bridgette's heart. She would always feel some level of responsibility for the miscarriage, but knowing in her heart that her sister didn't blame her would help Bridgette to heal from the loss and move on. The only question lingering was would she be moving on with or without her husband?

Chapter Forty-Two

Bridgette wanted to pounce on Nick for what he was doing at this moment. Her heart ached at the confusion followed by the pain etched on her sons' faces. They were visibly upset at what Nick was saying, but she'd agreed to keep her distance, though she hadn't gone far. She watched them from the kitchen as they sat out on the deck, and Bridgette fought back tears a few minutes later as she watched Dylan, her oldest twin jump up from his seat, his expression twisted in anger and his face wet with his own tears, swing the French doors open and race past her.

"Dylan, baby," Bridgette called after her now, nine- year-old son, but she heard his angry footsteps stomping up the stairs. She glared at Nick when he glanced at her as he held Ryan who was also crying. Bridgette felt hatred toward him that she'd never felt before, even though she knew this was probably the best decision right now. They certainly couldn't continue how they had been, but it still hurt nonetheless that they were separating, even more so for her children.

She'd been with the man almost eleven years; their wedding anniversary was in a few months. It was just a sad end to what she thought had been a good marriage, even though Nick had claimed otherwise. Bridgette still couldn't comprehend the things he'd said to her a week ago after she'd confronted him about the lease she'd found. It was almost as if he was saying to her that for most of their marriage, he had been unhappy and Bridgette wouldn't accept that.

Bridgette rolled her eyes at Nick, shaking her head and then headed upstairs to check on her son. She found Dylan in the center of his bed with his knees up to his chest, his arms wrapped around his legs and his face buried in his lap, crying. She sat next to him and enveloped him in a hug, placing a kiss on his head.

"I know it's going to be tough, sweetheart because you're used to Daddy being here in the house with us, but everything is going to be okay. We'll be okay. I promise you that, baby," said Bridgette.

Dylan continued to sob. "I don't want him to leave. I don't want to live here either if Dad doesn't," Dylan sobbed.

"Honey, you'll still be able to see him and spend time with him," Bridgette said.

"But it won't be the same, Mom."

"Sweetie, sit up and look at Mommy," Bridgette urged her son, pulling his arms apart and placing her hand on his chin to lift his head to face her. She wiped his face with her hands, even though his tears continued to fall. His pain pierced her heart and Bridgette wanted to cry too.

"You're going to have to be a big boy for Mommy now, sweetheart. I know you'll miss your Dad, but sometimes mommies and daddies have to have some time apart from each other. You know how when you fight with your brother I have to separate you two so you can cool off?"

Dylan nodded.

"Then once you've had time apart, you come right back together like brothers should because you still love each other, right?" Bridgette continued.

"Yeah. I guess so," Dylan murmured, sniffling.

"Well, me and Dad need that same time, even though we still love each other," Bridgette said. "You understand what I'm saying, honey?"

Dylan nodded again.

"You know me and Dad love both you and your brother more than anything in this world. That'll never change and your Dad leaving has nothing to do with either of you. It's just grown-up stuff, okay?"

Again, Dylan nodded, though Bridgette wasn't sure if he was quite satisfied with what she was telling him. But, it was all she had because the future regarding the Harper family was unknown.

Bridgette didn't know if she and Nick's separation would be temporary or permanent, and the latter disheartened her. She knew her boys would be affected tremendously, and she didn't want to think about it, but she had to face the truth. She could end up being a divorced single mother, which was something she'd never imagined, and the same for her marriage. Who would've ever thought that they would be here?

Chapter Forty-Three

Ivy stood in the bakery section at Publix; pondering over what baked good she wanted to indulge in. She would do anything right about now for a slice of Bridgette's German chocolate cake, and her sweet potato pie for that matter. This was one of the effects of pregnancy that she hated, and why she looked like the Goodyear Blimp, but if she didn't satisfy these cravings, her crankiness would be on a hundred. Savannah had fallen victim to it the other day, and Ivy felt bad afterwards, but she hadn't bothered to apologize to her sister because she couldn't promise that it wouldn't happen again.

Savannah was being a pest, and for good reason, but Ivy just didn't have the patience for it anymore. Her threshold had reached its limit. Pregnancy hindered what little filter she had, but if you asked Bridgette, her sister would say she never had one. She could recall Bridgette being the same when she was pregnant with Dylan and Ryan, but she seemed to forget that.

She'd called Ivy to reprimand her for speaking to Savannah the way she had and urging her to apologize. Ivy wasn't surprised. In fact, she'd expected it because that's what

Bridgette did, made everyone else's business her own, which is why Ivy was in the predicament she was now.

If Bridgette would have just kept her nose out of Savannah's marriage and hadn't felt the need to fix her fertility problem, then she wouldn't have set this chain of events in motion. Ivy would be in Paris now working with one of the top fashion designers in the world instead of being stuck in Atlanta while her figure burgeoned. Ivy knew it was irrational thinking, but that's how she felt. It was another big opportunity she'd had to pass on that would've taken her career to another level.

Ivy finally settled on a box of assorted doughnuts and a half of a chocolate cake. She would've love some red wine to go with the chocolate, but she'd have to settle for almond milk, which she needed to get, so she pushed her cart toward the dairy section. As she made her way in that direction, she stopped when she saw him and thought about going in the opposite direction before he saw her, but it was too late. He already had.

He was standing at the counter of the fresh seafood department. A smile spread across his face as he waved at her. Ivy waved back, but she was reluctant to move. She didn't know whether to go over and say hello or wobble back from which she came. But she wouldn't have to decide because he was headed her way.

"So, we meet again. How are you?" Kean asked her, his eyes resting briefly on her belly before returning to her face.

"Well, considering the circumstances," said Ivy and he chuckled.

"I'd say so. Pregnancy seems to agree with you. You look radiant," he complimented her, which made Ivy blush. But, he'd always had that affect on her.

"Thanks for saying that, Kean. Even though I feel the opposite."

"You've always been beautiful, and I don't think that could ever change. Your baby's father is a lucky man," he said, his voice showing a hint of disappointment and Ivy's smile disappeared. She hated lying to him, and now she questioned if she wanted to keep lying. His light brown eyes that always mesmerized her told her the answer.

"About that. You see—," Ivy began.

"Daddy, we found the salad dressing and Mommy let me get Cookie Crisp this time." Marley ran up to them, holding up the box of cereal. "Hi. I remember you. You have a baby in there," she said, pointing at Ivy's stomach.

Ivy smiled. "Hello, princess. And I certainly do." Ivy rubbed her stomach. A few seconds later, Marley's mother, Octavia walked up with a bottle of salad dressing in her hand.

"Hello," she said to Ivy, smiling at her.

Ivy returned the gesture. Octavia was looking just as cute and fashionable as she'd seen her the last time, in a sunny-yellow dress and brown wedge sandals. Her natural hair was tied into a neat bun at the top of her head. Ivy couldn't help but to feel fat and frumpy in her presence. She'd never been the jealous type, but there was something about Octavia that made her feel that way. Maybe it was because of her past relationship with Kean, and now she questioned whether Kean had been with Octavia the entire time they'd been seeing each other. But, it didn't matter now or did it?

"Hello, Octavia. I love that dress by the way. I can't wait until I can get back into my regular clothes. At this stage, all I'm comfortable in are stretch pants and sneakers. Neither of which I would've been caught dead in before," Ivy said, resting her hand on her stomach. Octavia chuckled. "Thank you. And I certainly remember that feeling, but from the looks of it, you won't have too much longer. Do you know what you're having?" she asked.

"Don't know yet. We're going to wait until the delivery date."

"How exciting. Well, whatever you're having, I'm sure you're going to love being a mother. It's the most rewarding feeling in the world," Octavia said, cupping Marley's small, round face, making her giggle.

Ivy's only response was to smile because she had no words. Again, she didn't want to have to lie.

"Mommy, I want a baby too. I want somebody to play with," Marley announced.

Octavia glanced at Kean and the awkwardness between them wasn't lost on Ivy.

"Well, baby girl, you'll have to talk to your Daddy about that one," said Octavia and Ivy made that comment her cue to escape.

"It was good to see you all again," said Ivy, making eye contact with Kean before averting her eyes back to Octavia and Marley. "Enjoy your cereal, princess," she said to the little girl with the complexion of a shiny, new penny who smiled her snaggle-tooth smile and then Ivy headed toward the dairy section. She glanced back briefly to see Kean's eyes still on her. She'd wanted to tell him the truth about her pregnancy, but she was glad for the interruption. It was obvious that he was a happy family man now so it didn't matter whether he knew or not. And for some reason, the thought of him with Octavia bothered her.

Ivy had always been forthcoming about wanting to keep their relationship somewhere between platonic and intimate. Even though they'd never had sex, they had developed something more than a friendship. She didn't know how to define it or if it was even important to, but she was feeling some type of way about seeing him with his daughter's mother twice now. They were definitely a couple and it bothered Ivy. Maybe it was the hormones of being pregnant or a reality that she was being forced to face, but she couldn't help but to wonder if Kean was the one she'd let get away. That was surprising to her because she hadn't been looking for "the one".

For years, she'd battled being in committed relationships versus staying single, but still dating—the latter winning out most of the time. She didn't deal well with the lies and deceit being in relationships often brought, at least the few she'd been in, so she'd opted to date for pleasure and fun, and if they had money that was even better. She wasn't a gold digger and never had been because she did quite well for herself, but she did like nice things and it was always a plus when she didn't have to spend her own money, and that was just being honest. And Kean Hawkins certainly fit that criterion.

She missed their late night chats when they were both away due to their careers, and their trips together to some of the most exotic places in the world, but mostly being in his presence. She loved his native New Orleans accent and how he challenged her every chance he got, whether they were discussing pop culture, sports or politics, it always made for a great debate. She didn't know what it was about Kean, but he sparked something in her that she'd never felt with any other man. She couldn't explain it, but she was almost certain that she probably would never have that feeling again. And she was okay with that or was she?

Chapter Forty-Four

"Do you think I'll be a good mother?" Savannah asked Julius as they enjoyed an alfresco dinner out on the deck. Spring was in the air again and it was the perfect evening to watch the sunset over the horizon of the lake. Julius had prepared blackened salmon over a bed of yellow rice with a zucchini, squash and carrot medley, and they were sharing a chilled bottle of pinot grigio.

"You're going to be an excellent mother. That I'm sure of," said Julius.

"How can you be so sure? I can't even cook a decent meal," said Savannah, a concerned look on her face.

Julius chuckled. "Sweetheart, don't concern yourself with that right now. That won't be something you'll have to worry about doing for a while anyway since the baby will be drinking formula for the first year," said Julius, cutting into his salmon with a fork.

"I know, but I want to learn. I know I'll never be a great cook like you and Bridgette, but I want to be able to make the basics that are kid favorites like spaghetti and fried chicken," said Savannah, sipping from her wine glass. "That's why I begged Bridgette for Mama's old recipe book. I'm going to practice."

Julius smiled. "Well, I applaud your enthusiasm and determination. I'll be on hand to help if you need me. You know I could've been the next chef G. Garvin," he joked, winking at her.

Savannah chuckled. "You certainly could have been. Maybe I'd be able to have you around more if you'd been a chef," said Savannah, her eyes fixed on his.

"Come on, baby. Let's not start this again. We're enjoying a nice dinner and evening," said Julius, wiping his mouth with a linen napkin.

"And we are, but I'm only saying what's true, Julius. When was the last time we've been able to spend some quality time together like this?" Savannah asked.

"It doesn't matter, babe. What's important is that we're doing it now," said Julius.

"But, it matters to me. So, please don't try and negate my feelings because you don't deem them as important as I do," said Savannah, her appetite waning by the second.

Julius sighed. "That's not what I'm trying to do, sweetheart, but we've had this discussion before. Well, several times. And it's beginning to get a little redundant," he said.

"Redundant? Really, Julius? Well, what's *redundant* is all of the time I seem to be spending alone. We have a baby coming and I don't plan on parenting alone. We're both going to have to make some sacrifices," Savannah huffed, letting her fork rest on her plate. Her appetite had dissipated and now a bitter taste was forming in her mouth. She hated to argue with her husband, but some things had to be addressed.

As newlyweds in their first year of marriage, they'd already been through more than a couple married twenty years. And if they were going to make it further, they would have to be on one accord, which they hadn't been. They both had great careers that could be demanding at times, but they'd always been able to find a balance, but in the past few months, that had changed.

"And I don't dispute that, Savannah, but if I want my practice to expand on another level, I have to put in the work. We've been doing well these past few years, but I want better. And maybe you can focus more on being home than working," he said and Savannah glared at him like he'd called her out of her name.

"Meaning what exactly?" Savannah asked.

"*Meaning* that you can stay at home with our child. You've always wanted to be a mother, so that can be your focus and not having to work," said Julius.

"So, let me get this straight. You want me to be a stay-at-home mother while you fulfill your dreams of becoming the next Johnny Cochran? I don't think so."

"That's not what I'm saying at all. I'm only putting it out there as an option. I know how much you love being a principal and how hard you worked to get there, and how remarkable it is to be in that position for someone your age. I would never tell you to give that up," he said.

Savannah softened her stance. She reached for his hand across the table. "I'm sorry, honey. I don't mean to jump on you, but I miss you when you're not here and it gets lonely in this big house by myself. I just want you to be cognizant of that. All I'm asking is that you manage your time a little bit better."

Julius smiled, but it didn't reach his eyes and Savannah knew that she'd upset him and ruined their evening. He moved her hand to his lips and kissed it before setting it back down.

"I'll clean up out here if you want to just go on inside and relax," he said, rising from his seat.

"Would you like some dessert?" Savannah asked, trying to hide her disappointment. She didn't want their evening to end. There was no telling when they'd get another. "I picked up dessert from Sugar Rush. Italian Cream cake."

"Maybe later." Julius picked up their soiled dishes from the table.

Savannah gently grabbed his wrist to stop him. "Or you can have me for dessert instead? A little brown sugar," she said in a seductive tone.

They still faced a few challenges in the bedroom since her surgery, and even more so after she'd been thrown into menopause not long after chemo and radiation treatment because her ovaries had been damaged as a result, so vaginal dryness was an ongoing issue for her. But, they still managed to get back to an active sex life.

"That sounds tempting, but I think I'm going to turn in early tonight. I have a long day ahead of me tomorrow and have to be in court first thing in the morning." He walked back inside the house carrying the dishes and leaving Savannah feeling heartbroken and rejected.

She bit her bottom lip to prevent herself from crying and prayed that they weren't heading down the same path as Bridgette and Nick. And certainly not with them getting ready to be parents. That would be a travesty, and something she wouldn't be able to deal with, especially after everything else she'd been through.

Chapter Forty-Five

Bridgette made sure the boys were away because it was the day Nick was moving out of the house. They were spending the weekend at Savannah and Julius's, which they always enjoyed. Bridgette would have liked to be somewhere else too, but she wanted to make sure Nick didn't take anything from the house that he wasn't supposed to. She didn't want to be petty, but she'd paid for a lot of what they owned, and she wasn't about to sit by and watch him walk out with any of it. He made the choice to leave his family, so as far as she was concerned all he'd leave with was his clothes if she had anything to say about it. And, she was going to have the locks changed as well. Since he wasn't going to be living there, he certainly didn't need a key.

Nick had been carrying boxes from the house and loading them into a small U-Haul truck early that Saturday morning when Bridgette had gotten up to shower and have breakfast. As she made a bowl of oatmeal, she thought about how Nick would survive since she had always cooked for him. And it was funny for her to imagine him over a stove. She honestly had no idea if he could cook or not because she had never witnessed it. But, how or if he ate would be no concern of hers anymore. It hurt that it had come to this moment, but she would have to continue to pray about it because there was nothing else she could do other than beg him to stay, and that wasn't going to happen.

Bridgette had just poured a glass of grapefruit juice and was headed back to the kitchen island to sit and eat when she heard voices coming from the foyer. She thought maybe Nick had gotten some of his buddies to help him move, but then the voices sounded muffled as if whoever was talking was now whispering and curiosity caused her to go check. Bridgette walked out of the kitchen and headed to the foyer, but froze when she heard her mother-in-law, Cassietta's voice.

"Mama, please keep your voice down. I don't need any trouble today. I told you to wait at the apartment," Nick was saying to her.

"Well, I'm a grown woman and I won't be told what I can and can't do. Who does she think she is anyway, forbidding me to come here? That hussy got some nerve. Now, get out of my way, Nicholas. I'm here to help you get your things out of here as fast as you can so you can be done with that dry cake-making witch," Cassietta huffed.

Bridgette felt herself getting ready to go from zero to one hundred, and she took a deep breath to calm down because she didn't want to have another altercation with her mother-in-law. But she wasn't going to sit back and listen to her insults while she was standing in her house.

"Ohhh, if it isn't the Queen of the palace herself, speaking of the She-Devil," Cassietta remarked when Bridgette stepped into view.

"It's great to see you too, Cassietta," Bridgette replied with sarcasm. "Hope you won't be here long."

"Don't try to be cute with me. I hope you're happy now that you've finally managed to run your husband away. Good luck in that cold bed at night," Cassietta retorted, her face twisted into a smirk.

Nick placed his hand on his mother's arm. "Mama, come on. We're going back to the apartment. We're not going to do this today," he said, and Cassietta snatched her arm away.

"Oh, I'm just getting warmed up, son. I've sat back and watched this heifer make you look like less than the man you are and it makes me sick, especially when you've always been a good husband and father," she said to Nick in a disgusted tone. "But, you always reap what you sow, honey. God don't like ugly and that's why you're paying in full now," Cassietta said, glaring at Bridgette. "And it started with that baby you was carrying around. It was ungodly how it was conceived and it's unfortunate because an unborn child is innocent, but that miscarriage was a high price you had to pay."

Bridgette felt the heat rising in her like a volcano about to explode. She couldn't believe her mother-in-law could be so nasty. It was a low blow even for her. They'd never had the best relationship, but it had never been this bad either. They always managed to tolerate each other for the sake of being in-laws and because of her love for her grandchildren, but Bridgette didn't have to do it anymore.

"Don't you ever speak about my miscarriage again. Do you understand me, Cassietta?" Bridgette glared at her, placing her hand on her hip and she could tell Nick was getting nervous. He certainly didn't want a repeat from last year.

"Mama, I said let's go," he demanded, reaching for her arm again, but Cassietta moved out of his grasp and closer to Bridgette.

"Who do you think you're talking too? I can talk about what I want to, especially when I'm speaking the truth. You better get on your knees and pray for repentance because the Lord is going to keep coming down on you," Cassietta said, pointing toward the hardwood floor for emphasis.

"Mama, please. I'm not going to say it again. Let's go. Now," Nick urged, keeping his eyes on Bridgette as her chest heaved because he knew she was about to go off. He grabbed his mother's arm and gently nudged her toward the door.

"Gladly. I've never liked this big, flashy house anyway. Like the house your Granddaddy left you wasn't good enough to live in for her Highness. She had to slap you in the face once again by buying something bigger and grander. What a dishonorable and disrespectful thing to do. Always trying to keep up with The Joneses. But, I hope you like living in it by yourself. Witch," Cassietta hissed before marching out the front door.

Bridgette inhaled deeply and then let out a long breath. Nick stared at her with an apologetic look. She knew he was about to apologize, but she put her hand up to stop him.

"Don't, Nick. Just go. Get her off of my property before things get ugly. That woman gets a kick out of pushing my buttons and I hate that I continue to let her get to me. And she's right about one thing. I do need to pray, but not for the reasons she said, but that I don't end up in jail and you sitting in front of her casket," Bridgette said, rolling her eyes.

"I didn't know she would come here, Bridgette. If I had known I would've tried to stop her. I don't like seeing you two at each other's throats," said Nick with a pained look in his eyes.

"Well, I don't know what you expect me to do, Nick when she's continually disrespecting me. The things that came out of her mouth were uncalled for and nasty," Bridgette said, shaking her head. "She was being mean and just plain evil."

"I can't control what comes out of my mother's mouth, but I'm sorry she said those things, especially about the…you know?" Nick said, and Bridgette knew that he didn't want to say anything about the miscarriage because he still felt guilty about it

"Just go, Nick."

"I'll be back tomorrow for the rest of my things," he said, before turning to leave.

"You know I have church tomorrow, so that's not going to work. I prefer that you just get everything out today because I have a locksmith coming to change the locks later," she announced, causing him to turn back around to face her.

"Well, I guess I'm not surprised. It is *your* house."

She didn't like his tone and she felt like he was piggybacking off of his mother's comments about her buying a bigger house. "Nick, just for the record, I've always considered this house to be ours. I've never tried to make you feel otherwise, so I don't know why you've had such an issue. What was so wrong about wanting something bigger for our family? And plus, your grandfather's house is still in your family. That's why you rented it out," she said.

Nick shook his head. "No. It's not. I sold that house four years ago, Bridgette," he said, his voice lowering.

Bridgette looked at him in shock. "What? Why would you do that?" she asked, her brows furrowed in confusion.

He was silent a few seconds before responding. "To help you start your business, but just like with everything else, you found a way to exclude me," Nick murmured and then turned to walk out the front door. "I'll be back in a few hours for the rest of my things," he said over his shoulder, closing the front door behind him, leaving Bridgette standing in the foyer shocked and confused.

Chapter Forty-Six

Bread of Life Baptist Church was abuzz with praise and worship as the choir belted out the ending to "We Come This Far By Faith". A chorus of "Amens" and "Hallelujahs" spread throughout the sanctuary. Savannah was in tears as she dabbed at her eyes with a handkerchief, moved by their uplifting performance. Julius had been holding her hand and gave her a comforting squeeze as she composed herself. Bridgette was on her feet in the pew in front of them with her children, her arm and hand extended in praise.

Reverend Barrett stood at his place on the pulpit, waiting patiently for order to be restored as he always did when the congregation broke out into a frenzy, which happened often during the two-hour time frame of service.

"Let the church say, 'Amen'," Reverend Barrett's voice boomed through his microphone, five minutes later as the commotion ceased.

"Amen," the congregation complied in unison as Reverend Barrett prepared to give his sermon.

Everybody listened intently as he spoke about family and going through adversity and healing after. Bridgette openly shed tears as she thought about what her family had been through over the past year, but she took comfort in Reverend Barrett's inspirational words. Her mind went to her husband and their fractured marriage, and as she glanced at her boys sitting next to her, her oldest twin, Dylan's hand rested on top of hers to comfort her, she prayed for discernment.

Had she done the right thing letting Nick leave so easily without putting up a fight? Maybe she should've suggested that they seek marriage counseling. It was obvious there were issues that she'd overlooked and Nick had been harboring resentment because of it. Yes, he could've said something to her, but would she have really heard him with the way she'd submerged herself into running a successful business while still trying to maintain their household? His biggest gripe was always that she did too much, especially for everyone else. She'd almost gotten herself killed trying to protect Ivy and put her life at risk again, getting pregnant for Savannah, and she'd managed to damage her marriage in the process.

As she sat hearing Reverend Barrett's baritone voice as he preached with passion and conviction, she realized that Nick had a right to be angry with her and in his feelings about their marriage. She'd put him in situations unwittingly because she hadn't considered how her actions would affect them both. They were supposed to be a unit, but she'd been acting in the singular. It all made so much sense while listening to the word of God, but sometimes tragedy had a way of bringing what was truly important to the forefront. Her eyes and ears were wide open now.

∽

"Bridgette? The rolls. You're going to burn them. Now, I may not be much of a cook, but I know they're looking awfully brown," Savannah interrupted Bridgette's thoughts a few hours later.

They'd reconvened at Savannah's house after church for Sunday dinner. Bridgette's mind had been consumed with thoughts about her marriage, and it was hard to focus on much of anything else.

"Shoot," Bridgette exclaimed as she hurried to the oven.

Savannah had been making a salad while she'd been making a pitcher of sweet iced tea. "Are you okay, sissy?" she asked as she watched Bridgette don an oven mitt and pull the bread out.

Bridgette was reluctant to mention anything regarding Nick because she knew how Savannah felt about him. She still blamed him for the loss of her baby and had refused to be anywhere near him. Their altercation at the hospital had been the last time she'd seen him, and that was over a year ago.

"Other than trying to get used to the idea of raising my sons in a single parent household, I couldn't be better," said Bridgette, removing butter from the refrigerator.

"I'm sorry, Bridge. I hate that you're going through this. Despite my feelings about Nick I can't celebrate the dissolution of a marriage," said Savannah. "And, I feel responsible."

Bridgette popped a bowl with a half stick of butter in the microwave to soften it.

"Well, don't. I'm the one who offered to be your surrogate. And, I don't regret that decision." Bridgette leaned against the counter waiting for the timer to end.

"Everything you did was for me and if it wasn't for that fact this probably wouldn't be happening. Your separation, I mean," said Savannah, stretching plastic wrap across the wooden salad bowl.

"Savannah, neither one of us knew this would happen. It's unfortunate, but I don't want you to keep blaming yourself." Bridgette pulled the butter out of the microwave when it dinged and then spread the yellow, oily liquid on top of the warm bread with a brush.

"While that may be true, I still can't help but to feel like I've turned everybody in my family's life upside down in one way or another. And while I'm eternally grateful to you and Ivy for putting your lives on hold to give me the ultimate gift, I feel guilty sometimes for the sacrifices you've both had to make," Savannah lamented.

"Savannah, we're family. And that's what we do for one another. I saw a way to help and I did. And like I've told you time and time again, I'd do it all over again. The exact, same way. I have no regrets because I would do just about anything for my family, except kill somebody."

"Thank you for saying that, Bre. And I feel the same about you and Ivy as well, even though she hates me right about now. I really hoped this experience would draw us closer like we used to be, but she seems to want nothing to do with me. And, I can't help the uneasy feeling I have," said Savannah.

Bridgette poured them both glasses of her freshly brewed, sweet iced tea and brought them to the island. She handed one to Savannah before taking a seat next to her.

"She doesn't hate you, Savannah. This is a new experience for her. We've been through it before, so we knew a little of what to expect, but I don't really think Ivy realized what she was getting herself into. She's used to being on the go all of the time, wearing what she wants and doing what she wants. Being pregnant has halted all of that, and she's having culture shock or in her case, baby shock."

"I hope that's all it is. I've tried talking to her about it on numerous occasions, but she always shuts me down before I can get a word in. I just want this to be over for both of our sake," said Savannah, sipping from her glass and then giving Bridgette a thumbs up signal to let her know that she approved of the sweetness level.

"It will be in a few, short months. And then maybe after the baby comes and you get acclimated to motherhood, we can spend some quality sister time together at the beach house since we haven't been there in ages. I think that's what we all need."

"I do too, and especially being at the beach house. We haven't been since we were there to see the completed renovations," said Savannah.

"Almost two years," said Bridgette.

"Wow. I didn't realize it had been that long. But, life has a way of making you lose time," Savannah murmured.

"So true. Time is the one thing that none of us have, so that's why it's so important for us to get back to the basics of what made us such a tight knit family. And our parents' beach house is the perfect place. It's truly home for us and the one place where their spirit really surrounds us," said Bridgette, smiling at the thought.

"I agree," said Savannah. "It'll be good to go back."

"Mom, is it time to eat yet? I'm starving," Ryan whined, walking into the kitchen. Bridgette and Savannah chuckled.

"I'd thought you'd still be full from all those blueberry pancakes you ate this morning that your uncle made for breakfast," Savannah joked.

"That was hours ago, Auntie Savannah. I'm ready to eat again," Ryan replied, rubbing his stomach for effect.

Bridgette tousled his soft hair, cut into a Mohawk style young boys were wearing now. "Dinner will be served in a minute, sweetheart. Why don't you and your brother go get washed up and then let Uncle Jules know we'll be ready to eat shortly?"

"Is Dad coming too?" he asked, and Bridgette felt a tug at her heart as she glanced at Savannah who gave her a sympathetic look.

"Not this time, honey."

"But, why? He said that we're going to still see him like always, and we always have Sunday dinner together," said Ryan, his voice sad.

Bridgette hugged him close to her. "Well, he's very busy this weekend, but maybe you can give him a call later."

"Okay," Ryan responded, even though he still wore a sad expression.

Bridgette placed a kiss on his forehead and sent him off to get ready for dinner. "This is going to be harder than I thought," she remarked to Savannah who reached over and gave her a much-needed hug.

Chapter Forty-Seven

Three months later…

On a balmy August evening at 6:55 p.m., Arianna Elizabeth Yancey was delivered at Piedmont hospital in Atlanta, weighing in at seven pounds and four ounces. Ivy had been in labor almost sixteen hours with her sisters and Julius there for the delivery. Baby Arianna was a chubby cheeked beauty with a head full of black, curly hair. Ivy marveled at the fussy newborn from her hospital bed as the neonatal nurse cleaned and dried her under a warmer. Savannah cried tears of happiness while Julius embraced her, both proud new parents hovering close by.

Bridgette stayed by Ivy's side and held her hand, which she'd done throughout the entire delivery, and when the baby was placed in Savannah's arms instead of hers, Ivy felt a piercing in her heart that brought tears to her eyes. She knew the day would come when she would have to part with the baby, but she'd been the one carrying her for nine months and there was no denying that a bond had been formed.

"You did a great thing, Ivy. I'm so proud of you," Bridgette whispered to her as she embraced her.

"I just want a chance to hold her for a few minutes, Bre. Can't I do that? Just for a few minutes?" Ivy pleaded.

Bridgette wiped Ivy's tears with her hand. "Honey, you know that's not what was agreed upon. I know it's difficult and I understand that you've carried her and naturally you feel a connection, but it's important that Savannah starts the bonding process."

Ivy's only response was more tears. Although they had signed a surrogacy agreement with strict stipulations, that still did little to comfort Ivy. It was just a piece of paper, and it didn't negate her feelings. Yes, biologically she was Arianna's aunt, but the bond that she'd formed with her was motherly. She'd spent months nurturing her and learning what made her react in the womb. Arianna knew her as mother, and not Savannah. It didn't seem like a fair exchange, even though she knew what she had signed up for. This was going to be harder than she could've ever imagined.

"I don't know how I'm going to do this, Bre. Pray for my strength," Ivy murmured as she glanced over at the happy, new family moment Savannah and Julius were having with Arianna who seemed to be content in Savannah's arms because she'd stopped crying.

"Of course, sweetie," Bridgette said, placing her hand on top of Ivy's. "It's already done. And, you'll just take it one day at a time. I'm a mother, so I understand exactly what you're feeling. But remember the blessing that you wanted to give to Savannah. You've accomplished that and you should be proud of that. I know our parents would be." Bridgette smiled as she glanced over at the new parents with their baby.

Everything Bridgette conveyed to her was the truth, but Ivy still felt a compelling sense of loss, and she didn't know how or if she'd be able to be in the background of Baby Arianna's life when she'd been such an integral part of hers. Tears came again as she watched her with her new mother—from a distance.

Chapter Forty-Eight

otherhood wasn't what Savannah had pictured it to be. It was harder than she had imagined. She seemed to be having a difficult time bonding with her daughter, and it was frustrating her because she didn't know what she was doing wrong. Arianna cried all of the time, and it seemed to Savannah that it took forever to calm her down.

They'd been back in Charlotte a few days, having left Atlanta right after both Ivy and Arianna had been released from the hospital. Bridgette had decided to stay a few extra days with Ivy, which Savannah thought was a good idea. She would've liked to also, but she had to get back home and begin a routine with her new baby. And, as usual, Julius needed to get back to work, which annoyed Savannah. She felt like if she could take time off from work to bond with their daughter, then he should have to. But, he'd promised that after he wrapped up the current case he was working on, he'd take a few weeks off, so she didn't make a big fuss about it. Still, she wasn't happy. As she feared, it felt like she was parenting alone.

Savannah was the one who had been getting up with Arianna while Julius slept peacefully, calling hogs along the way with his snoring. Savannah felt like smothering him with a pillow, as she snatched the covers away from herself and planted her bare feet onto the hardwood floor. The clock on the nightstand read 2:02.

The sound of her baby's cries blaring from the monitor next to the clock summoned her to Arianna's nursery. She turned it off before heading there so Julius wouldn't be awakened, even though he was usually a hard sleeper. She knew he had an early start that morning, so she was trying to be considerate, but she felt like cracking him over the head with it. It didn't seem fair that she should be the only one tending to their baby.

"Okay, sweetie. Mommy's here," Savannah spoke gently to her daughter as she scooped Arianna out of her crib and cradled her in the pink blanket she'd laid on top of her when she'd put her down to sleep four hours earlier. Arianna continued to cry and squirm in Savannah's arms.

"Awww…sweetheart. I know. Let's go to the kitchen and get you a bottle," Savannah said, trying to calm her down, but as usual it wasn't working.

Thirty minutes later, Savannah was the one in tears as she held her daughter who had calmed down some, but was still cranky and whiny. Savannah rocked with her back and forth in the rocking chair in her nursery, and she felt like the worst mother in the world. Arianna just didn't seem comfortable in her arms. She always squirmed and was irritable until she eventually drifted off to sleep from her exhaustion of what Savannah felt was Arianna fighting her love—rejecting her. And the thought hurt Savannah to her core.

She thought motherhood would come naturally no matter how Arianna was conceived and brought into the world. Savannah had no doubt that her motherly instincts would kick in and her daughter would take to her, but obviously she'd been wrong and she didn't know how to deal with that.

She'd never had a problem bonding with other people's children. She always had a nurturing spirit because of her innate desire to have children of her own. Her nephews loved her and the many young students that surrounded her daily at the elementary school adored her. So, why did her own daughter hate her?

Savannah looked down at her daughter who had finally drifted off to sleep and asked her that very question as if she could respond.

"Why do you hate me, baby girl? What am I doing wrong, sweetie?" Savannah cried while silently praying for a breakthrough with her daughter. It ripped her apart to think that her own child would never love her.

Chapter Forty-Nine

Ivy was glad to be in the sanctity of her home and away from all the poking and prodding of the doctors and nurses at the hospital. It had been a few days since she and the baby had been released, and while she was healing physically, emotionally she was a mess. It felt strange to have left home with a baby in her stomach and then return with nothing to show for it. She hadn't expected it to be this hard, especially since she'd always denounced motherhood. She'd only done the surrogacy thing to support her sister's dreams, but she would've never guessed she would feel such an emotional attachment to the baby. And yet here she was balling like one now because of it.

A stack of books she'd bought on pregnancy, when she first learned that she was, had triggered her tears when she saw them sitting on her coffee table. It had been the first time she'd ventured into the living room since being home, having spent the first few days in bed.

"Honey, it's okay to feel how you're feeling. It's completely understandable," Bridgette sat next to her on the sofa, rubbing her back.

Bridgette had found her crying when she'd come from the kitchen, having gone to make them some tea and popcorn.

They'd been planning to watch one of their favorite movies, *Brown Sugar*. Ivy was a huge Taye Diggs fan and Bridgette thought it would be fun to watch a marathon of his movies to try and lift her spirits, so they were going to watch *The Best Man* afterwards.

"I feel like a blubbering fool. I haven't cried this much in my life," Ivy sniffed.

Bridgette grabbed a tissue from the box sitting on an end table and placed it in her sister's palm. "You have to get it all out. It'll make you feel much better. You've always been the tough one, but everybody has a point in their life when they have to surrender to their emotions. And, I have to say, it's good to see you vulnerable. I knew you had a heart in there somewhere," she joked, pointing at Ivy's chest, bringing a weak smile to her face.

"I thought it would be easy since I never wanted to be a mother, but carrying Arianna really sparked something in me, Bre. I don't know how to explain it exactly," Ivy said, wiping her face with the tissue and then picking up a mug of tea and taking a sip. It was chamomile, just what she needed to relax her some.

"Are you saying that you want children now?" Bridgette asked, picking up her mug and taking a sip also. "Because if you are, that's going to go right up there with having a black president, something else I never believed would happen."

Ivy chuckled and she was glad to have her big sister there. Just a year ago, they couldn't be in the same room without bickering, but they were getting closer, and Ivy was glad about that. She was grateful that she'd wanted to stay a few extra days to make sure she was okay, but that was who Bridgette always was.

"I don't know what I'm saying. I guess I'm not as opposed to it as I was before," said Ivy.

"Lawd, hammercy. I might need to get up and do a praise dance," Bridgette joked and Ivy laughed.

Her mood was lightening up already. She knew that there were going to be tough days ahead, especially when she thought about the niece that she'd carried for nine months and then had to give away, but for right now, she was thankful to have her sister's support.

"Speaking of children. How are the boys dealing with Nick's absence?" Ivy asked. Bridgette was silent for a moment, and Ivy didn't know if it was a good time to bring up her brother-in-law since they were having such a light moment.

"They seem to be handling it pretty well. I think they've adjusted to not having him around on a daily basis."

"What about you? How are you dealing with it?" Ivy asked.

Bridgette paused briefly, running her forefinger around the rim of her mug as if she was pondering the question.

"Well, I won't lie. I miss him. A lot. It's been three months, but it feels much longer."

"Yeah, I bet. Especially when you're not getting any," Ivy remarked and Bridgette playfully tapped her on the leg.

"Ivy Lynne," she exclaimed.

"What? It's the truth. I've been a member of the same club for longer than I care to admit, so it's not like you're alone." Ivy laughed.

"Now, see that's the sister I know and love," said Bridgette, sharing her laughter.

"Seriously, Bre. I know how much you love Nick. I've never had a problem with him because he always seemed to show you nothing but the utmost respect and he's been a great father to my nephews. Now, he might've been a little old school in his thinking sometimes, but he's not perfect. None of us are."

"True. And I do love him. I've never stopped. Even with everything that we've been through. But, I don't know if that's true for him."

"Nonsense. That man loves you to the point of where it's almost sickening," Ivy remarked and Bridgette chuckled.

"It seems surreal that our marriage is where it is, but then again, so is everything else that has happened in the past year," Bridgette lamented.

"You're right about that, sissy," Ivy replied, reflecting on the major changes her life had underwent as well as she rested her hand on her now empty belly.

Bridgette noticed her gesture and rested her hand on top of Ivy's free one. "Well, the good thing about it is there's always tomorrow and therefore another chance to get it right."

"Yes. One of mama's famous sayings. And it's funny because they've come up a lot lately," said Ivy.

"I know. For me too. But, that's how I know she's always around. I feel her presence daily and it gives me comfort."

"Me too," said Ivy. "And, I know one thing she'd want."

"What's that?"

"For you to try and work things out with your husband. She loved Nick, and so did Daddy, especially when he didn't scare him off with that old rifle he used to pull out and sit across the kitchen table with every guy that we dated." Ivy laughed at the memory and so did, Bridgette.

"Oh my gosh. How could I forget? And, I tried to do the same thing with Julius when Savannah started dating him," Bridgette said.

"And it didn't work because he was laughing his butt off the entire time. But, he got the point though," said Ivy and they both laughed.

"Those were such good times. And what truly made us a family. We have to get back to that. I was telling Savannah that very thing a few months ago. That we need our annual family vacations to the beach house again."

"I really miss that place," said Ivy, thinking back to when she'd almost taken Kean there.

Ivy was certain that if they would've gone, that line between platonic and intimacy would have most definitely been crossed. There were only so much flirting, kissing, hugging and playful smacks on her buttocks that she could take. It was just human nature.

"Well, we should plan to go back soon. It'll be good for us," said Bridgette, smiling.

Ivy returned her smile, but she didn't respond. She knew that she wouldn't be around for a while and a family reunion wasn't going to happen anytime soon, but she didn't want to tell Bridgette that because she looked so hopeful.

Ivy had gotten a call from her agent the day after she'd returned from the hospital that she'd been anticipating, and it couldn't have come at a better time. She loved her sisters, but with everything she'd been through she needed some distance and to get back to what had made her happy in the first place—her career. And in two weeks, she'd be on a plane heading to Paris. Another opportunity had come up for her to work with that renowned fashion designer, and she wasn't going to pass it up this time. She'd be gone for at least six months, but she'd been seriously considering moving there permanently. It had always been a dream of hers to live in Europe, and now that she'd fulfilled her sister's dreams, it was time to get back to hers.

Chapter Fifty

Savannah just knew she was having a mental breakdown because she was dealing with some of the same emotions she had when she'd found out that she had cervical cancer and would be left barren because of it. She couldn't stop crying and she had a lot of anxiety. She wasn't getting much sleep because Arianna didn't seem to be either. Savannah would put her down to sleep, but she'd wake up crying a short time after. She thought something might be ailing her, so she'd taken her to the doctor a few days earlier than her first well child checkup, but the doctor had found nothing wrong. She told Savannah that some babies took longer to adjust than others, so it only confirmed for her what she'd already feared—that Arianna hated her. She never seemed to have the same reaction with Julius. It didn't seem to take much effort from him to calm her down.

Bone tired, and drained emotionally, Savannah didn't have the energy to get up when she heard her baby wailing from the speaker on the monitor. She ignored her, hoping she would just cry herself back to sleep since she didn't seem to want Savannah to touch her anyway. She knew it was irrational thinking, but Savannah was just too tired to care.

She loved her daughter, but motherhood had become a curse instead of the blessing she'd hoped it would be. Maybe there had been a reason why God had chosen to strike her with cervical cancer and take away her ability to bear children. She'd tampered with God's will and this was the result, so maybe Bridgette's mother-in-law had been right when she'd told Bridgette that. Savannah had thought it a cruel thing to say to someone, but everything that was happening was making what Cassietta said appear valid.

It was obvious that her daughter had created a bond with her sister, and the thought that she'd never establish the same bond was an indescribable pain that Savannah didn't want to face.

Arianna's cries had reached a grating, high-pitched level and Savannah turned the monitor off to silence her. Between Julius sounding like a John Deere lawnmower with his snoring and her baby's wailing, Savannah couldn't take it anymore. She needed an escape. She was unhappy with her marriage and motherhood. She had a husband who worked too much and a baby who had rejected her; neither seemed to care if she was around or not. This wasn't the life she'd dreamed about. It wasn't the life that she wanted.

Chapter Fifty-One

Bridgette was jarred awake by the ringing of a telephone. She didn't know if it was her iPhone or the cordless one to the landline because she was still in a slumberous state. She peered at the alarm clock on her nightstand. The illuminating numbers read 4:38, causing her to become more alert; a call that early in the morning couldn't be good. She shot up to a sitting position in bed, and when she realized it was her iPhone ringing; she grabbed it off the nightstand. Savannah and Julius's image filled the screen, one of many from their wedding that Bridgette had snapped throughout that day. Julius's name was displayed across the top, and she knew something had to be wrong.

"What's wrong, Julius?" Bridgette queried, her heartbeat starting to increase.

"Hey, Bridgette. Sorry to wake you, but I was wondering if you'd heard anything from Savannah or if she was there with you by chance?" he asked.

Bridgette could hear her niece crying in the background.

"It's okay, sweetheart," Julius said, trying to calm the baby down.

"No. She's not here. Is Arianna okay?" Bridgette asked. Her voice filled with concern.

"I think she will be. Her diaper is soiled pretty badly and I think she's been crying for quite some time now. Her little voice is hoarse," said Julius. "I looked every place in the house for Savannah and when I looked out into the garage, her SUV was gone. But, she left her cellphone here."

Bridgette could hear the worry in his voice.

"That's strange and it's not like her to just up and leave without telling someone, especially with the baby being there. Maybe she just ran to the store for something and was planning to come right back before Arianna woke up," Bridgette said, even though she felt an uneasiness nagging at her.

"I don't think that's it. Her purse is still here." Julius said.

Bridgette didn't like the sound of that, but she didn't want Julius to know that she was beginning to panic. "Julius, Savannah has a million and one purses. Are you sure she didn't just grab another one?"

"Well, I don't think so. Her wallet and other personal belongings are still in the one I've seen her carrying around lately. It's the lime green Michael something-other Ivy bought her for her thirtieth birthday last year. The one that matched one of their sorority colors," Julius said. Bridgette knew which purse he was referring to because she'd made a snide remark about it in jest at the time since both of her sisters were members of Alpha Kappa Alpha sorority.

"Maybe she just took some cash out the wallet instead of having to use her credit card," Bridgette said, unconvinced of her own words, but she had nothing else.

She ran through a list of places in her mind where her sister could be at that hour, but she came up with nothing because that was just something Savannah wasn't prone to do. Now, if it was Ivy that would've been more believable since that was the lifestyle she'd always lived, but her baby sister—there was no way. Something was definitely wrong. Her sisterly instinct told her so.

"I doubt it. She never carries cash. And now that I know she's not there with you and you haven't heard anything from her, I'm worried. I've never known her to do anything like this," Julius said, matching Bridgette's sentiment. She could hear him tending to her niece in the background and she seemed to be getting less fussy.

"I know. So you don't have any idea how long she's been gone?" Bridgette asked, adjusting the silk bonnet on her head.

"No. Once I pass out, I usually don't hear much of anything. Savannah always says that a tornado could swoop through the neighborhood and tear the roof off our house, and I'd still probably sleep through that."

Normally, Bridgette would have found his comment funny, but the fact that her sister seemed to be missing wasn't a laughing matter.

"I woke up to use the bathroom and I could hear Arianna crying from down the hall. And when I was done, it still hadn't ceased, so I decided to go check thinking maybe Savannah had gone downstairs to the kitchen to fix her a bottle, but she was nowhere to be found. I don't like this, Bridgette. Something's not right here, and I need to go find her and make sure she's okay," he said.

"I agree. The boys are with Nick this weekend, so I can come over and stay with the baby. Give me about twenty minutes," Bridgette said, already out of her bed and heading to her closet to find something she could throw on.

"Thanks, Bridgette," he said, and she could hear the weariness in his voice as if he was already thinking the worst.

"Don't worry, Julius. I'm sure there's a reasonable explanation for this. You'll find her and we'll all probably be laughing about this later," Bridgette said, praying that her words were true.

Chapter Fifty-Two

Bridgette was feeding her niece a bottle when Julius returned a few hours later. She'd met him in the kitchen where he'd entered from the garage, praying her sister would be with him. When she wasn't, Bridgette's worry had turned into fear. What if something bad had happened to her sister? She glanced down at Arianna, sucking her bottle, her innocent brown eyes staring up at her. And that thought ripped at her heart. Savannah had been through too much to bring Arianna into this world not to be around to watch her grow up.

"I've looked everywhere and there's no sign of her," Julius said.

Bridgette noticed how worn-out he looked. "I was praying she'd just return home before you got back. Where in the world could she be?" she pondered.

"I don't know, but I think I'm going to call the police. I've checked hospitals, the school where she works, grocery stores, every place I could think to look and I've had no luck. I've even been through her iPhone to see if I could find anything that might help," said Julius. "There's nothing."

"Julius, I hate to ask this, but I'm just trying to understand what could've happened to my sister. Did you have an argument or something you're not telling me about?"

Julius frowned. "What are you implying, Bridgette?"

"I'm just trying to figure out if there's something we're missing here. I'm not accusing you of anything sinister, but maybe she was upset about something and you hadn't noticed," said Bridgette. She removed Arianna's empty bottle from her mouth and placed her on her chest to burp her.

"We haven't argued about anything that would warrant her taking off in the middle of the night," said Julius, and Bridgette noticed the edge in his voice.

She really wasn't trying to upset him, but finding out where her sister could be was more important than his feelings. "Julius, I had to ask. None of this makes any sense. I'm worried about my sister and I pray that wherever she is, she returns safely."

Julius took a seat at the kitchen island and buried his face in his hands. "Savannah, baby. Where are you, sweetheart?" he asked. Then, his cell phone buzzed. Julius reached down into the front pocket of his blue jeans and removed it.

"What's up, DeShazo?" he asked the person on the other end.

Bridgette prayed it was some news regarding Savannah's whereabouts.

"What? Why?" Julius asked. His brow was furrowed and Bridgette moved closer to the island.

"Who is that? Is it about Savannah?" Bridgette queried.

"I'll be there in ten," Julius said, already on his feet and heading to the front door before he could end his call.

"Julius, who was that?" Bridgette asked him again. Her voice now irritated. "Was that about my sister?"

"It was Winston. Savannah's at his house. "I can't explain it now, but can you look after Arianna a little while longer?"

Julius was out the door before Bridgette could answer him or get any answers for herself. She was confused and annoyed that Julius didn't tell her where her sister was, but she was relieved that she'd been found.

Chapter Fifty-Three

Savannah had been driving around Charlotte aimlessly for hours after leaving home early that morning. She didn't have a specific destination, but she needed to be able to think clearly without the distractions that surrounded her at home. She'd finally ended up at Briar Oaks Elementary School, walking the empty halls and admiring the children's artwork that adorned the walls. It felt good to be in the place that she'd always felt so much love and respect, unlike when she was at home.

She'd sat in her office and laid her head down on her desk, crying until she didn't have any tears left. She didn't recognize her own life anymore, and that scared her. This should've been one of the happiest times because the one thing she had always wanted, she now had—her beautiful daughter. But, she was feeling like she'd made a mistake. She didn't feel like a mother, and she certainly hadn't acted like one this morning.

Savannah had ignored her baby's pleas to be comforted and abandoned her instead. Her daughter's cries met her as she walked down the hall, her nursery just a few feet away, and followed her as she descended the stairs to the garage to get into her SUV. Arianna's cries still haunted her as she sat in her office, and when she couldn't silence them, she felt the need to escape—again. But this time, she had a clear destination.

"Savannah? What are you doing here? Is everything all right?" Heather DeShazo asked her when she opened her front door thirty minutes later. She looked at Savannah's disheveled appearance and concern filled her face.

She'd thrown on a pair of black leggings, her sorority t-shirt and a pair of pink Tieks and her eyes were red and puffy from tears and exhaustion.

"I need to talk to you," Savannah murmured.

"Sure. Come on in," Heather said, stepping aside to let her enter the foyer. "What's wrong, Savannah?" she asked, closing the door behind them.

"Are Winston and the children home?" Savannah queried, looking down the hall.

"Yes, but they're all out by the pool. I was in the kitchen preparing lunch for later," said Heather. "How's Arianna? I've been meaning to come by and see her in person, but you know how busy we've been at the law office. I'm so happy everything worked out this time."

Heather had been the attorney to handle their surrogacy arrangement, both times. She was the third partner at the law practice that Julius shared with her husband, Winston.

"Well, that's what I need to talk to you about," Savannah said, averting her eyes.

Heather studied her. "Okay, we can go into the study." Her face was full of questions. "Can I get you anything?"

"No, thank you," Savannah said as she followed her down the hall toward the study.

"Is everything okay with the baby, Savannah?" Heather asked when they were seated on the large, sectional in the study.

"No. I mean, yes. I guess. I don't know, Heather. I've tried everything. I don't know what else to do." Savannah's eyes filled with tears.

Heather placed a hand on her leg. "What's wrong, Savannah? I know I'm your attorney, but I consider us friends as well. And we're sorors, so more like sisters," said Heather with concern in her eyes. "This doesn't have to be official."

"I can't do this. It's too hard," Savannah said, sobbing now.

Heather scooted closer to her on the sectional and wrapped an arm around her to comfort her. "It's okay, honey. Tell me what's going on? What's too hard?"

Savannah looked into Heather's hazel eyes. She'd always reminded Savannah of a younger version of Vanessa Williams. "I'm not cut out to be Arianna's mother. I can't bond with her. She hates me."

"Oh honey. Don't say that. Every baby is different. I know because I've had three. You have to give it a little time. She's only been here for about a week. She's still adjusting just like you're trying to. Trust me," said Heather.

But, Savannah wasn't convinced. "No. She hates me. She didn't grow inside me, so she has no connection to me. I don't know what I was thinking, but I made an awful mistake. I can't keep her."

"What do you mean you can't keep her? What are you saying, Savannah?" Heather asked.

"I think I should put her up for an adoption." Savannah's declaration caused a look of surprise to register on Heather's face.

"Why would you want do that?" Heather frowned.

"Because I'm a bad mother. I just abandoned my baby without a second thought. How could I do such a horrible thing?" Savannah sobbed. She was almost inconsolable as Heather tried to calm her down as she rubbed her back.

"What do you mean you abandoned her?" Heather asked.

"I just left her. She needed me and I left her." That thought made Savannah cry harder.

She could still hear her baby crying, and she would never be able to forgive herself for how she'd treated her daughter. She didn't deserve to be a mother for how she acted.

Chapter Fifty-Four

"Savannah, sweetheart?"

Savannah's head jerked in the direction of her husband's voice. She was surprised to see him standing there.

"Julius, what are you doing here? How did you know I was here?"

Julius stood with his hands buried in the front pockets of his blue jeans. Savannah could tell that he was just as tired as she was. His eyes were just as red as hers.

"Winston called," he said.

Heather looked just as surprised to see him as Savannah did. She rose from her seat. "I'll give you two some time to talk." She bent down and gave her a hug before leaving the study. She patted Julius on the shoulder before walking out.

Savannah wiped her tears with a tissue Heather had given her as Julius joined her on the sectional. He leaned over and placed a kiss on her forehead.

"Baby, I was so worried about you. When I woke up and couldn't find you, I didn't know what happened. I've been out of my mind all day looking for you. I'm so glad you're okay," Julius said.

Savannah saw the sadness in his eyes and it made her feel terrible.

"Julius, I'm not okay. I haven't been for a while, even before the baby came. And now that she's here, it's only gotten more complicated for me."

"Honey, I know you're feeling overwhelmed, but we're not putting our baby up for an adoption," said Julius and Savannah was surprised by his words.

"How do you kn—?"

"Winston overheard you talking to Heather, and he called me."

"Julius, I can't do this by myself anymore. I'm not equipped to handle all of this on my own," Savannah cried.

"I understand that now, sweetheart. And, I'm sorry that I haven't been present as much as I should be. But, we'll get through this together. We have a beautiful daughter that we've prayed about, and we owe it to her to try to be the best parents we possibly can be. She's going to grow up loving you as much as I do. You'll see," Julius said, grabbing her hand and placing a kiss on it.

"I'm sorry that I just left. I feel awful."

"Savannah, it's okay, sweetheart. You've been through so much. I think it might be a good idea for us to go and talk to someone—a professional. Maybe you're suffering from postpartum depression or something similar."

Savannah frowned. "How could I be suffering from postpartum depression? I didn't even give birth."

"I don't know, but something's going on and we need to find out what it is," said Julius.

Savannah was silent as she mulled over her husband's words. Maybe he was right. She at least owed it to him and her baby girl to find out. God had blessed her with what she'd asked for, and she had to have faith that he would work everything out for the better.

Chapter Fifty-Five

Two years later…

Savannah and Bridgette sat out on the beach, both of them stretched out in lounge chairs enjoying the view of the ocean and the twins, Dylan and Ryan, now eleven-years-old, splashing around in the water wearing their life vests.

"It's amazing how fast they're all growing. Time flies," Savannah marveled at the children. Arianna, who was inside napping at the beach house was now two-years-old.

"I agree," said Bridgette, flipping the page of her novel.

"Did you see that movie?" Savannah asked, from behind her sunglasses, pointing at the book.

"No. But, I saw Olivia Pope reading it when she was lying out on that island on that episode of *Scandal* when she'd run off with Jake. I bought it then, so you know how long ago that was, and I'm just now getting around to being able to read it," said Bridgette.

"We should go get it at Redbox to watch after dinner. Ben Affleck played the husband. *Gone Girl* was a good movie," said Savannah.

"Sounds like a good idea," said Bridgette.

"What sounds like a good idea?" They both looked up as Ivy walked up from behind them.

"We're talking about the movie, *Gone Girl*. Have you seen it?" Savannah asked.

"I read the book by Gillian Flynn and that was enough for me. That woman in that book was a special kind of crazy."

They watched her ease down in her chair. She was four months pregnant and wearing a bikini.

"Are you feeling better?" Bridgette asked.

"I'm fine, considering I look like an overcooked Butterball turkey," said Ivy.

"Oh stop it. I wish I looked that good when I was pregnant with the twins," said Bridgette. "And I certainly wouldn't have had the nerve to be parading around in a two-piece. Where they do that at?"

Savannah and Ivy laughed.

"Bridgette, you really need to stop watching all of those reality TV shows Fatima has got you hooked on," said Ivy. "You picking up too much of that ratchet lingo."

"I really do," Bridgette said, chuckling. "But, that's my guilty pleasure."

"Don't I know it? I can't get enough dark chocolate and red wine, of course. I sure wouldn't mind a glass now," said Ivy, licking her lips for effect.

"I'd swear you have stock invested in both," Bridgette teased.

" And speaking of chocolate, look at my Godiva chocolate drop out there looking like a *GQ* magazine centerfold," Ivy marveled as she watched her husband and stepdaughter splashing around in the water. "Seems like I get pregnant every time I look at that man."

They all laughed.

Ivy and Kean had been married for over a year now. They had a six-month old son, Elijah and now a daughter on the way.

When Ivy returned to Atlanta from Paris, deciding that living in Europe permanently wasn't something she wanted because she'd really missed her family, she'd run into Kean again at the Hartsfield-Jackson Atlanta International Airport in baggage claim. He'd been returning from Philadelphia where she now resided with him and their son.

She'd finally revealed to him everything about the surrogacy while having drinks at one of the restaurant bars in the airport, and he cleared up for her what she'd been wondering about his relationship with Octavia. They were just good co-parents for their daughter and they took her out occasionally for them all to do things together. Their relationship was platonic, ironically like theirs had been for so long. Octavia was now married herself, and they all got together from time to time for couples night and family night with the children when they visited Atlanta to see Marley. Octavia explained that she didn't want any more children and revealed that she had never planned to have Marley. Her and Ivy had become close over the past year.

"Look who's up?" They all looked back to see Julius coming toward them carrying Ivy's son.

"There goes my ba-byyy," Ivy sang her rendition of Usher's song to her child, which put a smile on his face as he reached out for her. She kissed him on the cheek and placed him on her lap, causing him to laugh. "Give me some of that Chunky Monkey," she teased the little boy, placing kisses all over his face.

"Dinner should be ready in about an hour," said Julius.

"Good because I'm starving," said Ivy. "And I know you put both of your feet in that meal you're cooking. I can't wait." They all laughed at Ivy and her voracious appetite.

A few minutes later, Nick came jogging up the beach clad in his running gear.

"What's up, fam?" he asked, planting a kiss on Bridgette's lips before dropping down beside her on a beach towel she had laid out for him. They'd opted not to divorce, but do marriage counseling instead. They decided to date and take their time getting to know the people they'd both fell in love with when they'd first married. He and Savannah had been working on their relationship as well. She'd apologized for attacking him in the hospital, and he'd accepted without hesitation. Now, they were all together at their parents' beach house on the North Carolina coast.

"Ain't no way I'd be out here exercising on vacation," Ivy said to Nick.

"Ivy, when have you ever exercised besides picking up a wine bottle?" Bridgette joked, making them all laugh.

"Moommm! Daaaddd!" Ryan came running up to them, breaking the camaraderie. "Dylan. He got pulled into the water. He took off his vest," he yelled in a panic. "I told him not to."

"Dylan," Bridgette screamed.

Nick took off running down the beach toward the ocean. He was already in the water before the rest of the adults got down to the edge. Kean and Julius went in after him as panicked screams filled the salty ocean air.

Chapter Fifty-Six

Bridgette placed a kiss on her husband's lips and slipped his wedding ring on his finger. It would be their final good-bye. As she took her seat back on the front pew at Bread of Life Baptist Church, between her children and her sisters, a primal wail filled the sanctuary. Bridgette sat stoic, but tears fell from her eyes as she tried to tune out her mother-in-law's cries.

If it wasn't her husband's funeral, she wouldn't have even allowed her children to be there, but it was their father lying in that casket, and after today, they'd never see him in the physical form again. They were visibly upset and Bridgette held each to comfort them as best she could. It was traumatizing enough, when Nick had moved out of the house, but how were they going to get past this. Her children didn't have a father.

"My baby, my baby," Cassietta screamed. "Why God? Why, my baby?"

Nick's brother Vincent and his wife, Yvette tried to hold their mother up as she flailed her arms and dropped to her knees in front of Nick's casket.

"Mama, get up. Come on," Vincent could be heard saying to his mother.

"What's wrong with Grandma Cassie, Mom?" Ryan asked her.

"She's just upset, honey," Bridgette responded. "She'll be okay." But, she was rolling her eyes on the inside.

"I'm scared, Mom. I don't want Grandma to die too," Ryan cried.

"It's okay, sweetheart. She'll be fine," Bridgette tried to assure her son as he clung to her even tighter. Now, she'd never tell anyone how to grieve, especially someone who had lost a child, but in her opinion, Cassietta was doing too much. All of the theatrics weren't necessary.

Bridgette closed her eyes and began to pray as her husband's casket was being closed. They would never get the chance to reunite as husband and wife. But, she knew that they'd see each other again. He'd lost his life trying to save their son's life. He'd drowned after getting pulled under by the same current as their son. His years of training in the water and being an avid swimmer, who was also physically fit, hadn't been able to save him. Thankfully, Kean and Julius were able to retrieve Dylan from the water before they were pulled further in by the current.

This tragic event would be something that they all would carry for the rest of their lives, but Bridgette hoped that they would be able to heal as a family, and not be drawn further apart. She knew how Ivy dealt with tragedy and loss, and she prayed that she didn't retreat and they not see her again for a long period of time, especially now that she had her own family. Bridgette wanted their children to grow up knowing one another.

Bridgette worried about Savannah the most. Savannah had never been quite the same after her cervical cancer diagnosis two years ago. And while she was still in remission, happily married and deeply in love with the baby she hadn't thought would love her back, she'd become guarded and overly protective. Bridgette worried how that would manifest itself later on in her marriage and as a mother. Julius seemed to be helping her through it.

When Bridgette opened her eyes, her mother-in-law was hanging on the top of Nick's casket, preventing the pallbearers from taking it out of the church. Vincent and Yvette were trying to pry her off, but weren't having much success.

"You can't take my baby. You can't take my baby," she yelled and Bridgette was disgusted at the spectacle she was making of her own son's funeral.

She decided she'd had enough as she rose to her feet and gathered up her children. They didn't need to witness their grandmother carrying on the way she was any further. It was too much; although, she felt at peace, assured that her husband was in a place much better than they were, hopefully with her parents.

"I'll meet you all in the car," she whispered to her sisters as she made her way down the side aisle, holding her boys' hands and averting her eyes as she walked out the front door of the church.

Chapter Fifty-Seven

The sisters got comfortable on Bridgette's red sectional as they all shared a blanket while they watched a TV marathon of *Golden Girls*, one of their favorite sitcoms. Savannah and Ivy had been trying to spend as much time with their big sister as possible since she'd buried her husband a week ago.

"Ivy, do you have to sing the theme song every episode?" Savannah asked, as Ivy belted out the last line.

"Of course, I do. That's the best TV show theme song that was ever created," said Ivy.

"Girl, bye as you would say," Savannah joked and they all laughed.

"Well, what's the best in your opinion then, Bubbling Brown Sugar?" Ivy asked, munching on red grapes after having remarked beforehand that they would be the closest thing to red wine she would get since she couldn't drink.

"I'll give you a hint," Savannah said with a grin on her face.

"As long as you don't have to sing it," Ivy retorted.

"Whatever. I can hold a note if I want to." Savannah rose from her seat on the sectional and then did her best impersonation of Sandra, the character from *227*.

"Maa-ry," she said trying to replicate the sultry character's voice.

"*227*," Bridgette guessed correctly.

"Okay, sissy. I can agree with you. That is a great one," said Ivy, and then she started singing the theme song. "There's no place like home, with your family around you you're never alone, when you know that you're loved, you don't to need to roam, 'cause there's no place like home."

"When I was at Grambling and I would watch reruns in my dorm room, I was always reminded of being home. And I remembered how much Mama loved this show. It was one of her favorites," said Savannah.

"I know. I really do miss those days with her and Daddy. But, that's why it's so important that we keep their memories alive and stay as connected with each other as we can. We've all been through some difficult times and suffered losses," said Bridgette, her expression solemn as she thought about her deceased husband. "But, we can never let those things knock us down or tear us apart. No more distance and no more fighting. Because as we all know, life is much too short."

"Yeah. Who would've ever thought that I would be somebody's mother or even a wife? I'm still wrapping my mind around that one, but I have to thank you both for that. Bridgette, if it weren't for you sticking your nose in Savannah's business like usual and offering your uterus up for rent, I would've never in ten million years have considered being a surrogate," Ivy said in the way only she could do it.

Savannah and Bridgette looked at each other and started laughing. Ivy was going to always be Ivy and nothing would ever change about that, but they wouldn't have it any other way. And as Savannah always said, she was in a league of her own.

"Carrying my niece and feeling her growing inside me was an experience that I would've never imagined, but it sparked a need in me to want to nurture, and now, I'm getting to do it a third time," said Ivy, placing her hand on her baby bump.

"I always said God has a funny sense of humor," said Bridgette.

"Indeed," said Ivy, rubbing her protruding stomach.

CPSIA information can be obtained
at www.ICGtesting.com
Printed in the USA
LVOW04s0045251016
510071LV00013B/176/P

9 781944 359195